ned

or

A DEATH IN THE ASYLUM

Euphemia, the disowned granddaughter of an Earl, is working as a housekeeper for Bertram Stapleford at his new property, when the dramatic collapse of the kitchen floor sends her back to where it all began, Stapleford House. A visiting mystic disrupts the Staplefords. Euphemia finds herself playing second fiddle to Bertram's new love, Beatrice Wilton, as she launches a project to investigate the new asylums. It is not long before she realizes that not only does Beatrice have her unscrupulous sights set on Bertram, but that her enterprises may be about to put them all in very great danger.

A DEATH IN
THE ASYLUM

by

Caroline Dunford

Magna Large Print Books
Long Preston, North Yorkshire,
BD23 4ND, England.

British Library Cataloguing in Publication Data.

Dunford, Caroline
    A death in the asylum.

    A catalogue record of this book is
    available from the British Library

    ISBN   978-0-7505-4236-4

First published in Great Britain 2013 by Accent Press Limited

Copyright © Caroline Dunford 2013

Cover illustration by arrangement with Accent Press Ltd.

Published in Large Print 2016 by arrangement with
Accent Press Limited

Magna Large Print is an imprint of Library Magna Books Ltd.

Printed and bound in Great Britain by
T.J. (International) Ltd., Cornwall, PL28 8RW

11914 6144

Chapter One

Calamity at White Orchards

Madam Arcana raised her face to the ceiling. Her large purple turban slipped dangerously backwards as she enquired in a loud stage whisper of the plaster above her, 'Is there anybody there?'

Despite the rather stern instructions I had been given to keep my eyes on the glass at the centre of the table I too looked up. But then very recently I had found ceilings to have become the most unreliable of objects.

White Orchards was not a large house. If Stapleford Hall is modest when compared to what my mother refers to as the "real great houses", she would doubtless rate Mr Bertram's new seat as adequate for an orangery and its flora incumbents, but never a dwelling for anyone who counted. This all despite the fact that since her marriage to my late father, the Very Reverend Joshia Martins, she had lived in a vicarage and since his death in a cottage that would have fitted neatly into the ballroom at Stapleford Hall and still left room to waltz around the perimeter. But then my mother still clings to memories of her youth in her father's – the earl who shall not be named's – great house. I have never seen my grandfather and now I am in service I doubt he will ever have the honour of meeting me.

Until last week, and the incident with the ceiling, I was a housekeeper at White Orchards. I had come to this position after many an unexpected turn in the previous 14 months. Having thrown myself into service in January 1910 to help provide for mother and my brother, Little Joe, when father left us destitute, fate had washed me up on the shores of Stapleford Hall the same day a murder was committed there. By the time the second murder had occurred – this time of the head of the house – I was entangled in the whole dreadful business and had made a dire enemy of the new Lord Stapleford and formed an almost inappropriate alliance with his younger brother, Bertram, who was quite the best of the family. Needless to say no one knew of my antecedents. Though I believe I was counted as somewhat of an oddity in a maid. I weathered these first two murders and their unfortunate consequences only for events eight months later to again take a turn towards the macabre.

The housekeeper, Mrs Wilson, had had an accident that I still cannot bear to fully recount. Suffice it to say that it involved the substance that comes from the more unfriendly end of a horse, very wet stairs and her sudden and ill-advised descent of the great staircase. This had led to a sudden promotion as I took on the role of housekeeper for a shooting party in the Highlands. I hesitate to say it, but again a sudden death greeted me almost upon arrival at the house. This time I clearly was in no way connected or suspected, but world events impinged on my tiny corner of England – or Scotland – and almost caused the arrest of our new, handsome butler, Rory McLeod. He was the son of a greengrocer, vastly ineligible, extremely intelligent and the main reason I accepted the post of housekeeper at White Orchards, when Mr Bertram declared his intention to buy his own house.

But I should have known things would not go smoothly. Mr Bertram is a passionate man and, like most hot-blooded men, he is quick to act. In the light of what was to transpire I believe that the purchase of White Orchards was itself a matter of impulse.

It is true I had challenged him on the morality of living in his brother's house merely to remain in the running to inherit Stapleford Hall as per the dictates of his father's bizarre will. I had also upbraided him on spending the blood money of the Staplefords (who are in banking and armaments) when he has a comfortable inheritance from his late godfather. However, when he stormed out in a rage at my impertinent words – and they were impertinent, even if my true social status had been acknowledged – I little suspected that I would set him on a course to buy almost the first house he saw and come running back to beg me to become his housekeeper.

At the time I knew in my heart of hearts it was wrong to accept. Mr Bertram and I – and this I only confess within these pages – are not indifferent to one another. There has never by word or action been anything improper between us, but I have often thought if I had not been a maid then Mr Bertram might have made his feelings plainer

– in a respectable manner. Of course, if I were not in service, and my real name acknowledged, he would be beneath my station to notice. I am not unaware of the irony of this situation, although I find no amusement in it.

And then there was Rory. Rory, who had every reason to believe we were on equal standing, who I rescued from wrongful arrest and whose quick thinking helped me untangle the most difficult of puzzles when Mr Bertram had set his face against aiding me. It was made plain to us, albeit individually, by the Staplefords that should Rory and I wish to wed the household would continue to employ us as a married couple, which was a very gracious concession, but that no extended courtship or close friendship was acceptable.

To be honest I think we were both taken aback as much by the sudden surprising morality of the Staplefords as we were with the suggestion that on a mere few weeks' acquaintance we would wish to wed. We chose to remain side by side in service, but with only a cool acquaintance between us. It was most uncomfortable. Mr Bertram had left and Rory was the sole person with whom I was able to engage my mind and active brain. We were naturally drawn together and I saw it would not do for many reasons, so when Mr Bertram returned I followed him to White Orchards as his housekeeper.

This is all a roundabout way of saying I leapt from the frying pan into the fire.

White Orchards was set with a most handsome facing, clean lined and modern on the fens. Sunrises and sunsets there were more magnificent than I have ever seen. It was surrounded by apple trees and when, in spring 1911, their white blossom flowered it was lovely to see. However a mere few months after our arrival, the floods began. An unexpected rainfall, a failing of some ditch and our basement was soon filled with water. However, I am always happy to rise to a challenge and now with my own small staff we weathered the storm literally and figuratively. We dried out what could be saved and threw out what could not. I was pleased with my adaptability and that I had not been thrown by this disaster.

However, when the event again occurred after just two weeks and then again, it became clear that unexpected rainfall or ditch failures could not be blamed. It was at this point that I enquired of Mr Bertram if he had checked with the local people about the house before purchasing it.

'I'm not sure I understand what you mean, Euphemia,' he had said when I presented him with his morning breakfast of eggs and toast.

'I mean, sir, did you realise the house would be liable to such flooding?'

Mr Bertram shrugged. 'It is in the fens.'

'I believe the engineering feat that drained the fens some time ago was and is regarded as something of a marvel,' I said.

'There are always teething difficulties when one takes possession of a new property.' Mr Bertram lifted his newspaper to signal the conversation was at an end.

'I think this is more than a mere inconvenience, sir. I fear there is a fault with the house that will need correcting.'

'Nonsense, Euphemia. It is a brand-new house. A marvel of modernity. The plumbing alone is a miracle.'

'Quite spectacular, sir,' I agreed. 'But it is the water outwith the pipes I am referring to. I fear the basement is flooded out again.'

Mr Bertram went pale. 'But my wines. My shipment. What I ordered laid down.'

'I'm afraid I didn't lay the wine down as per your instructions. I was confident that on reflection you would see it was an unwise choice.'

We were speaking to one another more formally than we had been used to at Stapleford Hall and even the wretched hunting lodge in the Highlands, but here, in the middle of nowhere – albeit a very beautiful nowhere - with a small staff we were thrown upon one another more often than either of us had suspected. I continued with caution. 'I fear we may need to quit the house while repairs are made. The smell from the cellars has risen in some strength to the kitchen and, as summer approaches, I fear it will become more rank. I do not think it can be sanitary.'

Mr Bertram pushed his plate away. 'So what do you suggest, Euphemia?' he said almost in our old manner.

'That we return to Stapleford Hall while repairs are put in process. I think, even if you wished it, in its current state White Orchards would not be saleable.'

'Damn it, Euphemia. I don't want to sell the place.'

'Then you will have to have it fixed, sir.'

Mr Bertram pushed his chair back roughly,

scraping a fine layer of wax off the floor Jenny had so lovingly polished. 'I will not believe it is that bad.' He stood and faced me angrily. 'I believe you are regretting your choice to come here and wish to return to work at Stapleford.'

'If you think that, sir, you must think me a fool,' I said as calmly as I could. 'What la-woman in her right mind would exchange the position of housekeeper for that of maid?'

'Perhaps you now find there are inducements at Stapleford Hall that White Orchards cannot supply.'

'Such as a dry cellar?'

'Enough! Show me the cellar. If there is more than an inch of water there I'll return to my brother's house tonight.'

'Certainly, sir.' I turned to lead the way out. 'Perhaps you should consider more appropriate footwear?'

Mr Bertram growled under his breath. He clearly did not believe me. We entered the cellar. I allowed him to go first. The dank, odorous water that seeped into the lining of his handmade shoes quickly changed his mind. 'Why didn't you tell me it was so bad, Euphemia?' he cried. 'This is impossible.'

I thought of responding that this was all of a piece. He had not believed me about the dangers of cracked eggs, the bad cheese from Hadwell Farm, the number of servants we would need and a thousand and one other things. Owning his own home had gone to Mr Bertram's head and each time I drew his attention to some shortfall he took it as a personal blow to his pride. For his own reasons he was utterly determined to demonstrate his mastery of all he surveyed. The result was, of course, that having lived all his life under his parents' roof he frequently looked extremely foolish – and then he blamed me.

'Shall I make the arrangements for leaving?' I asked. Unlike my master I had learned a great deal as housekeeper and was equal to much more than when we had first met. If anything this appeared to infuriate him further.

'We can't take all the servants to Stapleford!'

'No, of course not,' I replied. 'I suggest all the local servants are allowed home – although it will be very difficult to retain their service if they are not paid some kind of allowance.'

'That will be nothing compared to what this will cost to set right,' said Mr Bertram bitterly.

I moved on. 'I could return to my own home, but Merrit joined us from a London household.'

'Richard won't object to having another footman around as long as I'm paying.'

'I don't believe either Sam, the bootboy, or Jenny will have anywhere else to go.'

'Jenny?'

'Your kitchen-maid.'

'Oh, I'm sure Mrs Deighton can always use an extra pair of hands.' He frowned heavily. 'We can't take our cook!'

'Of course not, sir. I'm sure she will be happy to have some time to spend with her new grandchild.'

'Grandchild?' echoed Mr Bertram blankly.

'Your tenants, the Hadfields at Mile-End Farm.'

'Good God, Euphemia, you're my housekeeper,

not my...' He stopped, turned fiery red and swallowed. 'I mean, how come you know so much about my people? We've barely been here a moment.'

'It must be my background as a vicar's daughter, sir,' I said without thinking.

'But I thought your father was...'

'I'd better start seeing to the arrangements,' I answered and fled.

When we first met the Staplefords had assumed I was the love-child of some recently deceased gentleman because I spoke well and could read. At the time it had been easier to allow them to think this. 'Damn,' I said aloud, startling both the kitchen cat and cook in equal measure.

'It's not like you to swear, Miss St John,' said our cook, Mrs Tweedy. 'Has the master not seen sense yet?'

'Mr Stapleford agrees the house needs work and we are all to quit this place while it is done. All local servants will be kept on at wages, but allowed to go home. Merrit, Sam and Jenny will accompany Mr Stapleford to Stapleford Hall.'

'Well, that's very decent of him,' said Mrs Tweedy. 'And I'll get time to spend with the little 'un. But what about you, my dear?'

I blinked. 'I really have no idea.'

'Don't be stupid, Euphemia,' said Mr Bertram emerging from the cellar. 'Of course you're coming with me.'

He stormed out of the room. I followed. 'Really, sir, you mustn't call me by my Christian name in front of the other servants. It gives the wrong impression.'

Mr Bertram turned on his heel to face me. 'And what impression would that be, Euphemia? Apart from the ridiculousness of addressing one as young as you as Mrs...'

'Many women are married at 19,' I countered reasonably.

'But none of them would have the audacity to constantly contradict their master. You complain of my manners...'

'I meant simply that it might be taken as improper considering the isolated nature of the estate and you still a bachelor, sir.'

'Good God! You're doing it again. Will you not let me finish a sentence?'

I thought of pointing out that he had just finished two, but kept my tongue between my teeth. Mr Bertram heaved a huge sigh. 'And you're right again. I'm not fit to run a house on my own. I need a wife. Perhaps I shall find one at Stapleford Hall. Do you think along with all your other abilities to organise and correct my life that you might be able to find me a suitable spouse as well, Euphemia?'

'I may only be your servant, sir, but that is an unacceptable way to speak to me!'

By this point we were both breathing hard and our annoyance had brought us into close proximity.

'Euphemia, this has got to stop,' said Mr Bertram. 'Our relationship...'

Our eyes met, but whatever Mr Bertram was to say next was cut off by the sudden arrival of eight-year-old Sam hurtling round the corner.

'Is it true, sir, that you're taking me to the great

Stapleford Hall? Is it? Oh, sir, I'll polish all them boots better than anyone ever has.'

The moment shattered into a thousand pieces.

'Stapleford Hall isn't what most people would call great, Sam, but my elder brother would tan your hide for running around upstairs.'

'Oh lor',' said Sam stricken.

'It's a much more formal house,' I said kindly. 'But as long as you stay below stairs I'm sure you'll be fine. Mr McLeod, the butler, is a good man.'

Mr Bertram shot me a look of pure poison and strode off. This time I did not follow him.

It was at this moment of high personal drama that a loud crash echoed through the household. 'Dear God,' I cried and ran towards the sound with Sam hot on my heels.

I cannoned into the kitchen barely stopping in time to avoid falling through the large hole in the floor. 'Mrs Tweedy!' I cried in horror.

'I'm here, dear,' came a faint reply. Then slowly Mrs Tweedy climbed up the cellar steps. She was covered in dust.

'G-g-ghost!' squeaked Sam.

'Lord love you, Sammy boy,' said Mrs Tweedy in a shaky voice. 'It's just dust. I was checking to see what we could save from the waters when the bloody ceiling came down on my head.'

'Are you injured?' I asked in horror.

Mrs Tweedy shook her head. 'Gave me a bit of a fright, I can tell you, but that ceiling ain't no more than dust and plaster and we've been walking over it for months. This whole ruddy place is a death-trap.'

Mr Bertram arrived in time to hear Mrs Tweedy pronounce sentence. The look he gave me clearly suggested that he considered everything my fault. After all I had been the one who had urged him to buy his own home and I suspected in his eyes this made me ultimately responsible.

Less than 48 hours later I had completed our leaving arrangements. Mr Bertram and I were studiously avoiding each other, but there were still occasions when I entered a room too precipitously only to encounter one of his black looks before he exited smartly.

It was thus with a whole riot of mixed emotions tumbling through my head that I found myself approaching Stapleford Hall. This place had been the scene of much suffering and was still owned by a man, who if not evil incarnate, was at least of black heart. But it was also where my good friends Merry the maid, Mrs Deighton the cook and, of course, Rory McLeod lived and worked. My mother would be appalled that I considered those working below stairs infinitely superior to those above, but I believe my father would have understood.

I jumped down from the cart, which had conveyed me from the station, and made my way to the servants' entrance. As a housekeeper of White Orchards I felt no need to help with the baggage. The door opened before I reached it and two figures came out to greet me. I quailed inwardly. The servants' entrance at Stapleford was almost as large as our main entrance at White Orchards. I had forgotten how big the house was.

'Did you not bring any luggage?' asked Mrs Wilson, her black eyes snapping.

'I'm glad to see you are recovered, Mrs Wilson. The luggage is on the cart,' I said. 'Merrit, Jenny and Sam can bring it over. Although I daresay they would appreciate a little help.'

'Get it yourself. I'll not have airs and graces on my staff!'

'Mrs Wilson,' I said as diplomatically as I could manage. 'I am not on your staff. Mr Sta–Mr Bertram has arranged for three of his staff to help out with light duties as long as they do not conflict with our current duties. As a senior member of staff I have no more intention of lifting luggage than you would have.'

'Current duties! I daresay we can all guess what those might be.'

'I will be acting as Mr Bertram's secretary for our duration here,' I said through gritted teeth. I was so angry I managed not to blush while uttering the lie. What Mr Bertram had actually said as I was leaving the house for the train – he came by motor – was, 'Help out as you can, Euphemia, but don't let Wilson shove you back into being a maid. It wouldn't look good for either of us.'

Mrs Wilson muttered under her breath and turned away. It might have been 'Pah!' or even worse, but I closed my ears. I noticed she walked with a slight limp. She doubtless blamed me for her accident and I tried to find a charitable corner in my heart. I was still searching when Rory came up and offered his hand to me.

'It's gey good to see you, Euphemia.'

I took his hand in mine and smiled up at him.

19

Those luminous green eyes were as striking as I remembered and his bright blond hair shone despite the grey clouds overhead. 'It's good to see you too, Rory,' I said. 'How are Merry and the others?'

'Och, fine. Merry's been as nervous as a long-tailed cat in a room full of rocking chairs since she heard you were coming. Can't seem to make up her mind if you're liable to be friendly or all starched up now you're a housekeeper.'

'As if!' I exclaimed hotly. 'She is my dearest friend.'

'Aye, that's what I told her,' said Rory smiling. 'But you know Merry.' He paused and looked behind me. 'Who did you bring with you? Tell me you no brought your cook?'

I shook my head. 'Much as I love Mrs Deighton I wouldn't have dared,' I said. 'Most of our staff were local so we sent them home with wages, till the house is fixed. I've got Sam, Jenny and Merrit. Sam's from the local orphanage, a bit of a scamp, but grateful for the chance he's been given. He's bootboy at the moment, but he's bright and he'll go places. Jenny's our kitchen-maid. She's a good girl and a hard worker. Merrit's our senior foot-man. He'd be a butler if the place were larger and a London man, so we brought him down too. He's very eager to learn from you since when Mr Bertram enlarges his household he'll be in prime position to become butler.'

'You've no butler! Euphemia, you've been running that man's staff alone?'

'There's not that many of them.'

'That's not the point. You, a young woman, in

the middle of nowhere, running a bachelor's household. It's unseemly.'

'Oh Rory, please. It's been a long journey and I'm tired. You know full well that female staff under this roof have far more to worry about than any of Mr Bertram's ever will.'

'Not while I'm butler!'

'Maybe not, Rory. But you know Mr Bertram is an honourable gentleman.'

Rory bit his lip. 'Aye, well. Yer a grown woman and yer life's your own.'

'Please let's not fight. I've so looked forward to coming home and seeing you all.'

'Aye, well, come away in. Merry and Mrs Deighton have laid out a tea in the kitchen for you and your staff. Mrs Wilson's furious.'

The bright, modern kitchen was full of light and glorious baking smells. Mrs Deighton, cap askew, rushed forward. 'It's good to have you back, girl!' She hugged me hard. 'But you're all skin and bones. Where's your cook – I need to have a word with her.'

'In Norfolk,' I said. 'Merry, is that you hiding back there?'

Merry came forward shyly and I hugged her. 'I've missed you all so much.'

They both beamed at me. 'Sit down and have a cup of tea,' said Mrs Deighton, 'and tell us all about it. Is it true your roof came down?'

'I'll see to your staff and the luggage,' said Rory.

I sipped the very welcome hot brew and settled down to fill in Merry and Mrs Deighton on all the details.

It was considerably later when Rory came back

into the kitchen. 'Mrs D,' he said, 'our other guests will be arriving soon and I need Merry to make a last check of the bedrooms.'

'You have a house party?' I exclaimed. 'I'm so sorry. I wouldn't have taken up so much of your time. Mrs Wilson never said a word.'

'She's up with the Master and Miss Richenda. They've still not sorted out between them how long and what exactly this house party is,' said Mrs Deighton darkly.

'It's ever so exciting,' said Merry. 'Madam Arcana is coming – and Lady Grey.'

'Is it some kind of fancy dress?' I asked bemused.

Rory's grim face broke at that and he laughed out loud. 'Aye, you might say that. I'm sure Merry can fill you in on the details later. I hate to ask, Euphemia, but with Mrs Wilson closeted upstairs, I could do with a few things checked. Can you come with me?'

'Of course,' I said rising. Although I was puzzled as to how I could help. Rory knew his job far better than I did and was more than adequate to the task of compiling the most complex seating plan.

Rory took me into one of the smaller downstairs rooms – one of those sorts of rooms modern architects think look so good on plans, but for which it is difficult to assign a proper use. In the middle of the room the round library table from upstairs had been placed with many seats around the edges. In the very centre of the table was a crystal tumbler and scattered in a semicircle around the table on small cards were the letters A-Z and the words

'Yes' and 'No'.

'Oh no!' I cried.

'Aye, I'm not too keen on it myself. There's some things it's better not to be messing with, but Miss Richenda has ordered it.'

'Has she lost her mind?'

Rory gave a wry smile. 'It's not for me to comment on Miss Richenda's mental faculties, but if I were of a mind to do so I'd say that Lady Grey had more to do with this than a belief in ghosties.'

'Lady Grey? Does the house have a ghost? It's not old enough.' I frowned. 'Although it's seen more than its fair share of death. But I don't believe in these things, do you?'

Rory shrugged. 'My father always reckoned his mother had the sight, but I'm inclined to think this is more a parlour game to them upstairs than a serious effort to contact the dead.'

'What does Lord Stapleford think?'

'He's into pleasing Miss Richenda at present. He's hoping that if she's happy she'll look more favourably on his friend's suit.'

'Miss Richenda is getting married? But why would she want that? I thought the will said if she has the first child she gains possession of Stapleford Hall. Of course, I could have the details wrong.'

'Is that right?' asked Rory a shade more coldly. 'I'm not as conversant with the affairs of the family as yerself.'

I blushed. 'Rory, we need to talk. My taking the appointment at White Orchards was a big mistake.' I saw his face darkened and added quickly, 'Oh no, nothing like that. It's just that Mr

23

Bertram has never run a house before and his, er, impulsive nature makes me think he needs a housekeeper with a little more experience than me.'

'But where would you go?'

'I don't know,' I sighed. 'I'd like to come back here or rather go back in time to how things were.'

'Short of Mrs Wilson falling down another lot of stairs, Euphemia, I can't see that happening.'

'Neither can I,' I said sadly.

The door burst open and Miss Richenda sailed in. 'It's in here,' she called over her shoulder. She saw me and stopped short. 'You,' she said dramatically.

'I was just leaving, ma'am,' I said dropping a small curtsy.

A woman in her middle years and a huge purple turban with scarves trailing around her form like some plump and stunted maypole flowed into the room. 'But, my dear, you absolutely must not leave. There is an aura about you.' She turned to Rory. 'You, on the other hand, must leave at once. You are disturbing the spirits.'

Rory swallowed, nodded slightly and fled. I thought it most unmanly of him.

'Are you absolutely sure, Madam Arcana? This is a servant of my younger brother who is visiting with us a short while. I don't think I should trespass on his territory.' The words were sweet enough but the look she was giving me would have felled a horse.

Madam Arcana came close enough that I could tell she preferred sweet sherry to dry. 'Ah, but this one has been touched by death.'

'Marked by death?' asked Richenda in what I felt was far too hopeful a tone.

Madam Arcana laughed, a deep fruity sound. Although I thought her profession hideous I could not help but warm to her. I noticed for the first time her eyes were a peculiar but attractive shade of violet. Under the padding she had acquired over the years I could see she must once have been a very beautiful woman. 'No, no, Richenda. You are too fanciful.'

I felt this was a bit much coming from a medium. In the distance the doorbell rang.

'I detect that this woman has been around death – two, three, four times!'

That startled me. The deaths associated with the Staplefords were all too public knowledge, but she had counted my own private bereavement in her total.

'I do know a little of what I speak,' she said to me with a twinkle. Then she turned to Richenda. 'You see, the spirits are more comfortable around those who have been nearly involved in the demise of others. They become, if you will, guardians of the gateway.'

Richenda opened her eyes wide and, instead of decrying this piffle as I would have done in her place, clasped her hands to her chest and said, 'Oh, Madam Arcana, is that why I am sensitive? Because of Papa?'

Madam Arcana patted her arm. 'There, there. I don't know who told you that, but...'

The door opened to admit a familiar and most unwelcome figure. In his 30s, but already fleshy and wearing a vulgarly sharp suit, Max Tipton bounced into the room. 'Hel-looo!' he cried. 'Darling, you're looking sublime.'

For a moment I thought he was addressing Madam Arcana, but I could hardly have been more surprised when he grasped Miss Richenda's large and manly hand and pressed it to his lips. Miss Richenda simpered.

'Goodness, Baggy, do try not to be too sickening,' drawled a very well-bred voice. 'You'll put us all off our dinners. Tell him, Richie darling. He is just too, too much.'

A willowy female made her way into the room – sashayed is more the correct term. She had white blonde hair and was dressed richly and fashionably that gave everyone to understand she came from more money than any of us would ever see.

'Hallo, Beatrice,' said Madam Arcana with a smile. 'I see you finally got yourself invited to one of my sessions.'

Beatrice flounced over to a chair, looked pointedly at Baggy until he scurried over to pull it out for her and then leisurely sat. 'I'm here in my professional capacity,' she said.

'You're surely not expecting us to call you Lady Grey?' said Baggy. 'I mean, I respect your profession and all that, but you're not actually titled, are you?'

'I thought we were all using our professional names tonight. Or was I wrong, Agnes?' she shot at Madam Arcana.

The dressing gong sounded. Baggy laughed nervously. 'Saved by the bell, what?'

26

'Indeed, I must dress,' said Beatrice. 'Where is my room?' she demanded of me.

'I'm sorry, miss, I don't know. I will enquire for you.'

'Don't know! What kind of a ramshackle household do you run, Richie?'

Miss Richenda was forced to explain who I was and ended by saying, 'Madam Arcana has requested she be present at the séance tonight.'

Beatrice shrugged. 'If she's one of Bertie's servants she's hardly likely to be a plant.' She turned to give Madam Arcana a toothy smile. 'I must be on the lookout for anyone else with useful vibes. I'm sensitive myself.'

'You hide it so well,' answered Madam Arcana.

At this point I slipped out of the room and went to find someone to install Beatrice in her no doubt woefully inadequate chamber.

I helped as best I could as the household swung into action. After my long journey I was eager for my bed. Being not officially on staff I intended to head upstairs as soon as I thought Merry and Mrs D no longer needed me. I was therefore somewhat disappointed when Rory came to summon me.

'They want you upstairs at yon spook table,' he said.

'There's no need to look so disapproving,' I answered. 'I have no desire to attend.'

'Quite an argument about it, I heard, but Madam Arcana was insistent.'

'I'm not on staff.'

'Mr Bertram has endorsed it,' said Rory.

'What! He's involved in this charade?'

'The whole family are.'

'They must be mad,' I said with feeling, but I followed Rory upstairs. He didn't even come into the room, but ushered me in and closed the door.

Around the table sat Madam Arcana, Miss Richenda, Beatrice, Lord Stapleford, Mr Bertram, Max Tipton, two ladies I didn't recognise and Mrs Wilson. My jaw dropped.

'Opposite me, dear,' said Madam Arcana.

Mr Bertram and Beatrice shifted their seats to allow me in. They made an unfortunate couple. Mr Bertram looked somewhat sheepish and Beatrice mulish.

'Now we have our two independent sensitives present we can begin,' said Madam Arcana. 'If you will all place the index finger of your left hand on the glass in the centre of the table.'

'How bally exciting,' said Baggy.

'If I can ask for absolute silence? No one must remove their finger from the glass and no one must deliberately move it. I assure you I will know.'

Madam Arcana raised her face to the ceiling. Her large purple turban slipped dangerously backwards as she enquired in a loud stage whisper of the plaster above her, 'Is there anybody there?'

Under my fingertips the glass jerked and began to move.

Chapter Two

A Spirited Experience

'Good gad!' barked Mr Bertram.

My employer's startled exclamation brought me back to my senses. My father had lamented the foolishness of those using spirit boards, but he had never believed in them. Who should I trust now: the late Rev Joshia Martins or Madam Arcana? The answer was obvious. I lowered my head slightly, so I could appear to be watching the glass while watching the faces of the guests. Indeed no one needed to watch as Beatrice was loudly sounding out the letters. Her face was oddly pale and she was sweating unbecomingly along her top lip. Tiny tendrils of hair curled at her temples. Perhaps a man might have thought it becoming. I found her suspicious.

'H-A-R-R-I-S! Does that mean anything to anyone?' asked Beatrice.

Lord Richard shouted with laughter.

'Is he a relative of one present, who has passed over?' asked Madam Arcana in a soft but carrying whisper.

'It'd be nice to think the bug-blasted man was dead,' said Lord Richard, whose nose I now realised was ruddy with whisky drinking. 'But I expect he's off tormenting some other household.'

'I think, sir, if you have no objection I will

retire,' said Mrs Wilson. 'With the house at this level of occupation there is much for me to do to ensure yourself and your guests are adequately provided for.'

'Baggy, was that you?' asked Richenda and then to my surprise she laughed. 'You are a naughty boy! But such a scream!'

I looked in astonishment from Richenda to Tipton. Their eyes lingered on each other in a manner that was quite unsuitable so soon after dinner.

'Really,' said Madam Arcana. 'I understood this was to be a serious experiment. I am not some kind of circus act!' She was actually quivering with indignation. Did she believe this nonsense or was she annoyed at someone playing her at her own game? Mr Bertram met my gaze across the table and I could see he was thinking the same thing.

'Perhaps...' he began.

'Richenda! Control your guests,' said Beatrice. 'I too thought this was a proper experiment. And it is so rude to Madam Arcana to cheat.' She paused. 'Although I suppose it would make an interesting piece.'

All the participants went white as the ghosts they were trying to summon at this pronouncement.

'I'll behave. Word of honour,' said Baggy. 'This lark's all new to me. Just a bit on the nervous side. High spirited, don'cha know?' He laughed at his own joke and fingered his collar. 'Haven't broken it, have I, Madam A? Give it my full attention now. Word of a gentleman.'

I wasn't sure, but I thought Mr Bertram snorted slightly at this last pronouncement, but he may have been clearing his throat. Mrs Deighton had made her version of French chicken this evening and, much as I applaud her cuisine generally, even I had to admit it was unfortunately sticky.

Madam Arcana, who had half-risen, looked around the table. It might have been my imagination, but it was again Beatrice who appeared to have the most remarkable effect. 'If Miss Wilton, or should I say Lady Grey, wishes me to continue.'

'Only too eager,' said Beatrice sweetly.

'If you could all concentrate once more on the glass,' said Madam Arcana.

'Really, Lord Richard, I don't believe my presence is necessary,' said Mrs Wilson.

'Shut up, Wilson,' said Lord Stapleford.

Madam Arcana once more raised her eyes to the ceiling, severely endangering her turban. 'Is there anybody there who wants to speak to anybody here?'

Nothing happened.

'Is there anybody there?'

It felt as if we waited an age, but a collective hush had descended and no one appeared to be willing to break it. My left calf cramped, but I didn't dare move. Somehow as a group we had moved from doubt to expectation. I can only explain it by the lessening of light and encroaching indigestion.

I was going to have to stretch my leg soon or risk suddenly contorting in agony. If only I was taller and didn't have such short arms. I was at full stretch reaching out to the glass. Perhaps I could ease...

The glass jerked under my finger.

'W-H-Y-D-I-D-N-T-Y-O-U-W-A-N-T-M-E-M-U-M-M-Y. Why didn't you want me, Mummy?' asked Beatrice looking around the table. 'Has anyone here lost a child?'

'Not that I know of,' said Lord Richard.

'Dickie!' protested Bertram. 'There are ladies present.'

'Damn thing is nothing but a freak show.'

'If that will be all, Lord Richard,' said Mrs Wilson.

'If I have to stay, you have to stay,' said Lord Richard.

'Really, Lord Richard, I cannot see how this forms part of my duties.'

'Hush,' said Beatrice. 'The spirit may still be with us. The glass is warm.'

'By Jove, so it is,' said Baggy. 'I think we've snagged a live one!'

The glass began slowly to move.

'M-U-M-M-' said Beatrice.

Mrs Wilson shot to her feet, sending the glass flying across the table. The light in the room was dim, but to my astonishment I could see she was shaking. 'This is ungodly!' she cried. 'I will have no more of it.' She stormed out of the room.

'Good gad!' said Mr Bertram again. 'I've never seen Mrs W show emotion.'

'She certainly seemed upset,' said Beatrice. 'Did she and Mr Wilson lose a child?'

'It's a courtesy title,' said Richenda. 'As far as I know she's never been married, has she, Richard?'

'Shouldn't think she's ever even been kissed,' answered her brother. 'Let alone known a man.'

'Richard!' protested Bertram. 'You're drunk.'

'My house!'

'That's debatable,' said Richenda.

I slipped out of my chair. Not only was my leg very sore, but I had been a servant long enough to know any servant who observes their masters arguing is on a road to trouble. I had reached the door when Madam Arcana caught up with me.

'If you could point me in the direction of the small parlour?' she said. 'I was assured there would be tea waiting for me after the event. I do require some time in solitude to collect myself.'

'Of course,' I said. 'I'll show you.'

We crossed the black and white tiled hall, our footsteps echoing on the marble until we reached the swirling rug at the centre and both became quiet for a few moments.

'Ghastly thing,' said Madam Arcana. 'Poor Richenda has no taste.'

I smiled slightly. There was no way even someone who loved Miss Richenda could defend her taste.

'I know you think it's all a show,' said Madam Arcana as we entered the parlour. 'But the spirits are real.'

I smiled and nodded and made to take my leave. Madam Arcana caught me by the arm. It was not a bruising grip, but it was surprisingly strong. 'I saw you looking. That first time. Not watching the glass.'

'I-I didn't move it!'

'No, of course you didn't, dear. You clearly disapprove of such things. You have the look of someone brought up in a vicarage, which is why

33

I wonder if the message could be for you.'

'Message?' I said. Unruly hairs on the back of my neck were now standing straight up.

'Harris, the servant – that was one of the men. Heaven knows Lord Stapleford was drunk enough to do it himself, but Mr Tipton also strikes me as a foolish sort of young fellow.'

'Do you mean the message about the child?' I asked aghast, focusing on how this might relate to me.

'No, no. That was false as well,' said Madam Arcana waving her free hand dismissively. 'Really if people want to pay me money to watch them move their own glassware around the table it is their own business.' She released me and headed for the biscuit plate. 'Although, of course, if that's all that happens it can tend to give one a bit of a reputation. It's a pity Lady Grey was here. I was hopeful about that.'

'Beatrice? But Mr Tipton said it wasn't a real title.'

Madam Arcana sank down in a billow of scarves. A small smile played across her lips. She knew she had my interest. 'Beatrice Wilton. She's one of the Wilton newspaper family. They own them, of course, as opposed to write in 'em. Bea's the exception. They let her write a little column about gossip – Lady Grey's Notes. It gets her invited to all the right parties, which is all the Wiltons want, but Bea, if I'm not mistaken, wants a little more. I think,' she leaned conspiratorially forward and whispered, 'she might consider herself a writer.' She sat back, tutting and shaking a head. 'Very nasty for the family. Of course one knows writers, but no one wants one in the family.'

'What makes you think she has, er, aspirations?'

'Long words, dear. She uses long words. In her column and even over dinner. Not the done thing at all.'

'But surely if she's writing a gossip column she is a writer,' I persisted.

Madam Arcana took an enormous bite out of a biscuit and slurped some tea. 'Not the same thing. Ladies like a little gossip and like to see bits about themselves in the papers. Men, being the dominant gender or so we let them think, write news. It gives them the illusion that they run things. None of the Wilton papers would ever allow a member of the weaker sex to write actual news.'

'I see,' I said. Though it must have been plain I didn't. 'Anyway, if you have everything you need...'

'Oh yes, tickety-boo,' said Madam Arcana. 'Your Mrs Wilson has made the tea exactly to my instructions. Dry old stick, but she knows her job. Definitely a touch of the good stuff in this.'

I blinked and backed towards the door.

'Message, ah yes. These things sometimes come through to me. Especially when I'm focusing. Even if my attendees are up to their own tricks. An older man, kindly, vicarly, I'd say if pushed, but not on record...'

'A vicar?' I clenched my fists. Of course, if she'd been asking around the servants she might have heard reports I grew up in a vicarage. I'd been foolish enough to tell Rory that although it was at odds with what I had told the Staplefords. A horrible thought struck me – was Madam Arcana trying to blackmail me?

'Oh, they come through all the time. Terribly annoying. But as I tell them there's no point preaching. Stands to reason anyone in the room hasn't heeded the church's warnings or they wouldn't be there, so why they should listen to a clergyman just because he's dead… Though I suppose you'd expect them to have a better handle on how the afterlife works from a professional point of view. But honestly, they never have anything good for a séance. It's all about lost cats, elderly relatives and church roofs.'

'I don't work here,' I said trying to avert any attempt to winkle family secrets from me. 'I'm on Mr Bertram's staff. We were flooded out.'

'That explains why he was babbling about rising waters,' said Madam Arcana promptly.

I began to feel rather angry. The woman was definitely trying to trick me. I did my best to copy my mother's haughtiest expression. 'I strongly doubt the message was for me.'

'And if he doesn't think you're the image of your mother when you do that,' said Madam Arcana laughing.

'He's here?'

Madam Arcana shook her head. 'It's difficult to explain – especially to non-believers. It's more a sense of a person – an impression – and it tends to stay for a short while before it fades. But no, I wouldn't say he was here.'

'In that case,' I said opening the door.

'He said to tell you to beware your enemies.' Madam Arcana shook her head. 'No, that's not it.

36

He said: "Beware for your enemies". Doesn't make a lot of sense to me, but hopefully you'll figure it out. He seemed rather agitated about it. And there was a feeling too. Like something very bad was going to happen. But there you go. Spirits are always trying to put the willies up us mortals. I sometimes think it's the only fun they get.' She settled back against the cushions and closed her eyes. 'Probably nothing for you to worry about, dear.'

'No,' I said.

Madam Arcana opened one eye. 'I mean, it's not like you feel that too, is it?'

I didn't reply but closed the door quietly behind me. I made my way quickly to my chamber. As I undressed in the dark I found, to my annoyance, I was shaking. The wretched woman had been right. I couldn't put my finger on it and I certainly didn't believe it was anything to do with spirits, but from the moment I'd stepped through the portals of Stapleford Hall I had been experiencing a rising sense of dread and right now, as I blew out my candle, and sent my room into pitch blackness, I was so afraid of what was to come that my heart was hammering like a drum.

When I reached my long-awaited bed sleep perversely did not come easily. I must have been dozing when the disturbance came because I found myself halfway down the stairs before I was fully awake. Rory and I arrived in the hall at the same time. I blushed furiously. I had not thought to snatch up my dressing gown the noise had been so terrible and my nightgown was certainly not

37

adequate dress for an innocent nocturnal meeting. 'Did you hear that?' I asked, trying to cover my embarrassment. 'Someone is in terrible trouble.'

Rory's eyes flickered over my dress and he turned his head away. 'Euphemia, get back to bed!' he said.

At this point Mr Bertram appeared, running. He looked from one of us to the other and his face grew dark with anger. 'What are you doing...?'

He was interrupted by a crash and a cry, similar to the one that had awoken me. 'It wasn't a dream,' I said.

The sounds echoed around us in the large hall. 'Which way?' asked Mr Bertram, temporarily forgetting his righteous anger. But Rory had keener ears than either of us and he was already off, running towards the kitchen.

'Euphemia, stay here,' barked Mr Bertram and headed after him.

Of course I did no such thing. It was clearly a woman screaming and to be found in whatever dire predicament we all obviously feared without female support to hand was not to be thought of.

I pelted along the corridor. There was another loud cry and then came the sound of fighting. I realised it was coming from Mrs Wilson's room. But why would anyone... I had no time to complete the thought as a man in black with a scarf wrapped around his head appeared from around the corner. He was running at full tilt. I tried to dodge out of the way, but servants' passages are always narrow. I had one glimpse of glittering blue eyes, before I was roughly pushed aside. He caught me completely off balance. I staggered on the spot, trying to regain my balance, but my bare feet slipped on the tiles and I went down. My head met the wall and blackness overwhelmed me.

I came round to the sound of voices.

'Damn it, I had him,' said Rory.

'How was I to know?' snapped Mr Bertram. 'I was coming to help you.'

'And a fine help you turned out to be. I had him against the door if you hadn't opened it.'

'How dare you talk to me like this!'

'I'm no on yer staff. You let yon madman get away. Nay woman is safe in the household now. If he'd go after Mrs Wilson...'

'Quite,' said Mr Bertram in a very different tone.

'I'm thinking it was because she was on the ground floor.'

'Harder to sneak into the servants' attics, you mean?' said Mr Bertram. 'You have a point. Unless it was...'

'Seems unlikely, sir,' said Rory. 'After all, there is no one new in the house.' He paused. 'Other than your footman.'

'Merrit?' said Mr Bertram. 'Are you suggesting?'

'I'm suggesting it might be best to rule him out before the police get here and ask the same question.'

'Police?' asked Mr Bertram blankly. 'You called the police.'

'Yon doctor would have done it if I hadn't. It

looks better this way.'

'But he's been with the family for ever!' said Mr Bertram.

'Good God, man, he fair killed the woman!'

'Right. Right,' said Mr Bertram. 'Have you woken my brother yet?'

'I was just about to, sir, once we knew what the doctor thought and once we'd checked where your footman was.'

'I see. Thank you,' said Mr Bertram roughly. 'You appear to have thought of everything.'

'I endeavour to give satisfaction, sir,' said Rory with a notable trace of irony in his voice.

My eyelids felt extraordinarily heavy, but I managed to open them. I was lying on a chaise in the library. Rory and Bertram were standing by a roaring fire. I could see Bertram had a large brandy in his hand. Although to be fair he seemed to be holding it rather than drinking it. A heavy cover was thrown over me. I tried to lift my head and the world swam alarmingly. 'Is she all right?' I asked in what was admittedly a shaky voice.

Rory turned at once. 'Lay your head back down, lass,' he commanded. 'The doctor will be up to see you in a moment.'

'Honestly, Euphemia, what were you thinking of running around the household late at night, barely dressed?' demanded Mr Bertram.

I put my hand to my head and felt the large lump that was growing. 'I thought she'd need me after whatever...' I stopped as the words tangled.

'It was a right brave thing to do,' said Rory. 'Bloody stupid, but brave.'

'He knocked me down,' I said.

'Aye, you were lucky. He made a right mess of Mrs Wilson. Looks like he tried to kill her.'

'Good God!' I said horrified. 'Who was it? Have you caught him?'

'He was too fast for me,' said Mr Bertram, 'and Rory here was too caught up with carrying you upstairs.'

I gave Rory a weak smile. Mr Bertram glowered. 'Thank you,' I said.

'I thought for a moment he'd killed you,' said Rory, 'but looks like it's just a nasty knock on the head.'

'How did he get out?' I asked.

'Kitchen door and across the garden,' said Mr Bertram.

'Have you checked to see if everyone is where they should be?' I asked bluntly. (I can only offer the concussion as an excuse for my rudeness.)

Rory pursed his lips and shook his head.

'But it could be...' Sense returned and I didn't finish the sentence.

'Did you get a look at him?' asked Mr Bertram.

I closed my eyes and thought. 'No, I can't remember much. Only a black figure running and knocking me to the ground.' I opened my eyes again and the world swam alarmingly once more. 'I don't feel well,' I said.

'Where is that wretched doctor?' said Mr Bertram. 'Go and check, Rory.'

When we were alone Mr Bertram knelt down by my side. 'You gave me a terrible fright, Euphemia. You had no business ... unless you were with him when...'

'I was in my room,' I said coldly. 'Alone.'

Mr Bertram hung his head. 'It was finding you standing there with him, dressed as you were, and with all the commotion, I didn't know what to think.'

'You should know me better,' I said.

Mr Bertram's head hung a little lower. 'Euphemia,' he said, 'Euphemia...'

'Yes,' I whispered.

'There isn't any chance it was Merrit, is there?'

'Merrit,' I said flabbergasted. 'Why on earth would you think that?'

'He's new and Rory said the police would ask about anyone new to the house – either on staff or as guests. And apparently he's the only one.'

'Yes, of course. He's right. But can't you go and check if he's in his room? He can't be there and halfway down the park at the same time.'

Mr Bertram lifted his head and his clear, dark eyes met mine. 'It happened hours ago, Euphemia. You've been unconscious for ages. It took us a while to get the doctor and he's been with Wilson ever since. Rory's right. Whoever it was he tried to kill her and he did a fair job. I believe an ambulance has been sent for. Though why the wretched man hasn't been up to see you...'

Rory came back in and did a double-take to see Mr Bertram kneeling at my side. Mr Bertram hurried to his feet, brushing down his trousers and began blustering about the doctor.

'He is currently with a guest of Lord Stapleford's – Miss Beatrice Wilton. It appears the young lady is known for having a weak heart and has found the commotion she heard from her room most disturbing.'

Mr Bertram looked down at my dishevelled form. 'But Euphemia–'

'Is not a guest,' said Rory roughly, 'and the doctor has his orders, from Lord Stapleford himself.'

'By God, we'll see about that,' said Mr Bertram and strode out of the room.

Rory's face softened. He came over and very gently felt the lump at the back of my head. 'I've woken Merry and she's making you a cold compress. I didn't want to disturb you when you were out, but you're back with us now.' He smiled. 'Growing up I saw a fair few brawls. I donnae think you'll have much to complain about except a roaring headache for a few days.'

'The world's underwater,' I said plaintively.

'Aye, well, it would be with your brains all shook up. But you're talking fine and yer're alert and they're all good signs.'

Merry burst into the room, waving a wet rag around. 'Oh no! Oh, Euphemia! Are you dead?'

Even Rory chuckled slightly at this. 'Give that here, lass,' he said and tenderly placed the cloth on my head. The ache immediately subsided.

'Oh, thank you,' I said.

'You'll need to get a bucket with ice and keep rewetting the cloth until at least the doctor has seen her,' said Rory.

'Of course,' said Merry. 'You poor thing. What did the maniac do to you?'

'He knocked me down,' I said. 'We don't know if he was a maniac.'

'Who else could it be?'

'Mr Bertram is worried it might be our footman,

43

Merrit. Though he came with excellent refer-
ences.'

Merry shook her head vehemently. 'It weren't
him.'

'You're very sure,' said Rory curiously.

'We were walking.'

'Outside?' I asked.

'It's a full moon,' said Merry defensively. 'I got
into views when we were in the Highlands. I
offered to show the man some, seeing how he was
new to the area and a Londoner like myself. We
walked to the gates and back.'

'At night?' Rory frowned.

'It was proper,' said Merry with dignity. 'We
were both wearing our coats and everything.'

'Did you see the man?' Rory asked. 'The
maniac?'

'No,' said Merry. 'Should we have done?'

'If yous were out walking at the time of the
attack and the maniac didn't sprout wings and fly
over the wall, then, yes, you should have seen
him. There's no other way out of the park.'

'There must be,' I said. 'Loose rocks, a high
branch, some other way out.'

'We've got a new groundskeeper and he's very
good,' said Rory.

'But the gates would have been locked,' I said.

'Wrought iron gates aren't that difficult to
climb,' said Rory.

Merry grinned. 'Is that a confession of a mis-
spent youth, Mr McLeod?' She registered the
expressions on both our faces. 'I didn't mean to
be rude,' she said. 'I was trying to lighten things
a bit. The pair of you look like you've seen death

in the flesh.'

'Don't you see, Merry,' I said gently. 'If he didn't leave the grounds then he's still here. It could even be someone in the house.'

'Oh lor',' said Merry. 'Are they calling in the police?'

Rory nodded.

'Well, Lord Stapleford's going to have some explaining to do then,' said Merry.

'What do you mean?' I asked.

'Didn't you hear?' said Merry. 'He and Mrs Wilson were having the devil of an argument after that spooking session. Going at it hammer and tongs, they were.'

Chapter Three

The Return of Sergeant Davies

'You heard Lord Stapleford arguing with Mrs Wilson?' I repeated blankly.

'She was screeching her head off,' said Merry. 'I never heard nothing like it.'

'Not, of course, that you heard much,' said Rory. 'Just passing as you were.'

'Unless, of course, your bootlaces had come undone?' I suggested.

'Now you come to mention it I think that did happen.'

'Merry! Miss St John needs her rest and not a lot of silly nonsense.'

'Go on, Merry, it'll take my mind off my aching head.'

Merry looked from one of us to the other. Her emotions played so clearly across her open face I had to stifle a giggle. Should she indulge her love of gossip or please her new boss? Gossip won out, as I knew it would. 'She was complaining about the séance. Said how his father would never have exposed her to such a thing.'

'That's hardly surprising,' said Rory. 'It was an unpleasant thing to force any of the servants to do.'

'But she was really angry. Mrs Wilson doesn't get angry. Not with those above stairs – and there's more…'

Merry paused, savouring her moment. 'She accused Lord Stapleford of pushing the glass.'

'What?' snapped Rory. 'Are you sure?'

'She believes in ghosts?' I asked, confused. 'Did she think he was trying to tell us something?' My heart hammered at the thought of all the hidden secrets and buried bodies that the late Lord Stapleford had good cause to know of. 'Did she think he'd come back to tell the truth?'

'You must have hit your head awful hard,' said Merry. 'The only spirits Mrs W believes in come out of a bottle. No, you ninny, she said Lord Stapleford had exposed her to cruel and drunken antics and caused her pain beyond his meagre comprehension. What do you think she meant by that?'

'I have no idea,' I said quickly, although I suddenly had every idea. 'She sounds as if she was hysterical.'

'Aye,' said Rory.

'Oh, do you think so?' said Merry. 'But it wasn't like her.'

'She's a certain age,' said Rory darkly.

Merry looked mystified.

'Yer ken. The change of life,' said Rory and to my amusement he blushed deeply.

'I don't think she does, Rory,' I said.

Merry looked from me to Rory and back again. 'You must think I'm a right idiot,' she said. 'And if you're going to stay here Mr McLeod you can put the cloths on Euphemia's head. Likely, I'll have double the work tomorrow and I need my sleep.'

'Merry,' I gasped at such rudeness.

'Don't tell me you'd rather it wasn't this way, Euphemia,' said Merry with a twinkling smile. 'Get well soon.' And she tripped out of the door before Rory found his tongue.

'Well,' I said, 'when I left I thought she was getting rather fond of you.'

'Aye,' said Rory, 'She was.'

'What happened?'

'Yer brought yon footman, Merrit, with yer.'

'Oh, I am sorry.'

'I'm not,' said Rory. 'She's a grand lass, but no my type and yer ken how the Staplefords feel about relationships between their staff.'

I tried hard not to be pleased and failed. 'This thing with Merrit is very fast,' I said.

'London charm,' said Rory sharply.

'Unless he was using her?'

Rory opened his eyes wide then shook his head. 'Oh right, like that. I see what you mean. But if he was walking with her he couldn't be our intruder.'

'Nobody seems to have checked the times,' I said.

'The police will do that.'

We lapsed into silence. Rory changed the cloth on my head. As he leaned over me I saw those luminous green eyes were as clear and bright as ever. 'I missed you,' I said without thinking.

Rory sat back. 'And Merry,' I added quickly. 'It feels like coming home to be back here.'

'Aye, and with yon events like you'd never left, Miss Trouble,' said Rory with a smile. 'But you made your choice, Euphemia, when you went to White Orchards. It was a good choice. A promotion.'

'I didn't feel I had any other choices,' I said sadly. 'It's very difficult.' I felt a tear slide down my cheek. I brushed it quickly away. 'Don't take any notice of me, Rory. It's shock or something. My head is killing me.'

'I hope not,' said Rory taking my hand. 'Does Mr Bertram treat you well?' He frowned. 'He doesn't ... he hasn't?'

I shook my head and regretted it at once. 'No, he wouldn't. But we do have an odd relationship. He's so impulsive. It makes running the household hard. I never know from one moment to the next what he might require.'

'Aye, some masters are like that. They've no idea of the work they cause.'

'He didn't check out the new house properly. Any of the locals could have told him of the flooding. And then he wouldn't believe there was a problem. We argue all the time.'

'Argue?' said Rory. 'You shouldn't be arguing with your master.'

'I know, but we kind of got off on an informal footing when his father died and everything happened.'

'How informal?'

'Oh, for heaven's sake, Rory. There has never been anything improper between us and there never will be. Will you let that go?'

'You don't behave like master and servant.'

'No, we don't,' I said more calmly, 'and that is a greater problem than I had understood. Especially when we are thrown together so much at White Orchards. You're right, I should be more respectful, but if I didn't speak my mind he'd blame me even more when things went wrong. He relies on my opinion.'

'It sounds like a right mess,' said Rory.

'Yes,' I said miserably. 'It is. I should never have accepted the post.'

Rory squeezed my hand. 'Never mind, lass. It'll all come out in the wash.'

'That's what our old cook used to say,' I said sleepily. 'I don't see how.'

'Your cook?' said Rory startled.

'Ignore me,' I said quickly. 'It's that bump on the head. I don't know what I'm saying.'

Rory was giving me a penetrating stare. 'Is there something you'd like to tell me, Euphemia?' he said.

I was saved by the arrival of the doctor. As ever he was dressed in the same tweed coat. I looked at his worn face and made a discovery. 'I don't

49

know your name,' I said bluntly.

'Dr Simpson, Miss St John. I'm sorry to meet you again under such circumstances. Rory.' He nodded at the butler. Dr Simpson came and sat on the edge of the chaise beside me and took my wrist in his fingers. Rory let go of my hand and moved back towards the door. 'Yes, yes, leave us to it,' said Dr Simpson. 'I'll call if I need anything.'

Rory nodded and left.

'Good strong pulse,' said Dr Simpson. 'How do you feel?'

'A little sleepy and I'm saying silly things.'

'All to be expected,' said the doctor. 'I'm sorry I was so long getting to you, but you're a strong, sensible young woman. If it had been Merry now I'd have been more worried.'

'How is Mrs Wilson?'

'Away this good hour to the hospital.'

I frowned. It hurt. 'But why?'

'Beatrice Wilton needed my services.'

'Oh,' I said.

The doctor chuckled and asked me to watch his fingers as he moved them across my field of vision. 'I thought like you at first, but the young lady really does have a heart condition and a shock could have been most serious for her.'

'I'm the one who hit my head.'

'Yes, my dear, but you are a servant. Be grateful Richenda didn't demand I saw her friend before Mrs Wilson or the woman would be dead.'

'What about me?'

'You'll live,' said Dr Simpson. 'I'll tell them you need to be abed for a couple of days.' He looked

50

around the cosy library. 'Is that couch comfortable?'

'More than my truckle bed,' I said wryly.

'Right, I'll tell them you can't be moved for a couple of days. It'll let you get a decent amount of rest. To be fair it'll be a full week or more before you're back to normal. But I couldn't see why you shouldn't do light duties by the end of the week.'

'Thank you.'

The doctor started to pack up his bag. 'I'll leave a couple of fortifying solutions for you. Not that you're liable to need them, but it'll help convince the Staplefords to let you rest.'

'Will she live? Mrs Wilson?'

'I don't know,' said Dr Simpson. 'I've done what I can. Mr McLeod getting me so quickly helped, but whoever attacked the poor woman meant business.'

'Last time we spoke,' I said carefully. 'You said how you'd known Mrs Wilson since she came into service.'

'Hmm,' said Dr Simpson.

'You implied she had a secret.'

'You must be mistaken.'

'I know about the Hippocratic oath,' I said boldly.

'You do? Then you are the most remarkable maid – no, housekeeper now, isn't it?'

'I know you can't tell me anything.'

'Then you should know better than to ask.'

'Someone tried to murder her. Do you know why?'

'That bump on the head has given you the

51

strangest ideas. It's very common. They will fade by tomorrow.'

'There was a séance tonight.'

'So I heard,' said the doctor. 'Superstitious nonsense.'

'I agree, but I think someone interfered for their own ends. Someone very much alive.'

The doctor shrugged. 'House party games can get out of hand.'

'They made a suggestion using the table that someone present had lost a child. Mrs Wilson reacted very strongly.'

Colour ebbed from the doctor's face. 'They suggested she had a child?'

'No,' I said carefully. 'Not her particularly, but that someone present had lost one.'

The doctor said nothing.

'I remember when I first came here you tried to warn me – about the dangers of getting too close to the family. Only Mr Bertram is nothing like his father, is he?'

'No, he's not,' said the doctor and he closed his bag with a snap. 'I strongly suggest, Miss St John, that you turn your thoughts to more restful subjects. You've had a hard blow to the head and a severe shock.'

Our eyes met. The doctor was first to look away. I was almost certain I read fear on his face. 'Of course, doctor,' I said. 'I shall need all my energy when we return to White Orchards to set the house to rights.'

The doctor gave me a curt nod and left. I turned to look into the fire. As I watched the flames dance ideas began to form in my head. It seemed impossible, but it was the only thing that made sense. It had to be my concussion affecting my thoughts, because if I was right then any of the Staplefords could be Mrs Wilson's attacker. I breathed a sigh of relief. Except Mr Bertram. He had been with us. But what if they had hired someone else to do it? Behind me the door opened with a soft click. I froze. The Staplefords knew all too well how adept I was at putting together the pieces of unfortunate puzzles. So far we had reached a stand-off, but what if the events of tonight took that one step too far? What if the blow that had sent me reeling had been intended? What if I was next? I half-sat, half-twisted and fell off the chaise.

'Euphemia?' said Rory. 'Are you all right? I wanted to check if you needed anything before I went back to bed.'

He helped me back onto the chaise. 'I'm not surprised you're jumpy.'

'It's worse than that,' I said. 'I think I'm the next victim.'

Rory patted my hand as he drew the cover over me. 'Now, there's no need to fuss. I've checked the house is locked up myself.'

'But what if it was one of the family or someone they hired?' I asked.

Rory went over to bank the fire and then came and sat on a small stool in front of me. 'What's brought this on?' he asked.

'What Merry overheard Mrs Wilson say. I think I know what it means.'

'You mean you've put two and two together and made six.'

53

'What if she had a child?'

'I do follow you, Euphemia. I got the implication too. But what if she had a child with a Mr Wilson that no one remembers when she was very young? What if that child died? What if the late Lord Stapleford knew about it and she assumed his son would too? It's tragic, but infants die all the time. There doesn't have to be anything havey-cavey about this. It might not even have been her child. Perhaps her sister or even her mother had a child that died and it brought back bad memories.'

'The cards said "Mummy didn't want me". That's not the same as a child dying in infancy.'

'Yer telling me you believe in spirits?'

'Of course not. Someone present spelt out the message deliberately. They meant to cause trouble.'

'To highlight that they were going to launch an attack on the staff tonight?'

'No, of course not.'

'So you'd have the Staplefords or others deciding to hire someone to attack Mrs Wilson in the two hours after dinner and arranging to get the man here? It's not possible.'

'So you agree that it was her reaction to that message that led to her attack?'

'Och, Euphemia, I don't know. I need rest and so do you.'

'Dr Simpson said she had a child – Mrs Wilson.'

'He'd never have told you such a thing,' said Rory shocked.

'Well, no,' I admitted, 'but he implied it.'

'That's you and your bad arithmetic again.'

'You weren't there. He – he – tried to warn me before. Said he didn't want me to suffer the same fate.'

'Euphemia, you have a right bad tendency to go borrowing trouble. When will you learn that the only way to be a good servant is to leave them upstairs to their own lives? Don't get so involved.'

'We're all God's creatures,' I said quoting my father. I could feel my eyes closing.

'I sometimes doubt that,' said Rory and closed the library door softly behind him.

I awoke to find Merry re-doing the fire. Sunlight streamed in through the window. I winced and turned my face away. 'What would Mo-dame like for breakfast?' enquired Merry. 'A chicken wing and a glass of bobbly?'

'Bubbly,' I corrected. 'And what mademoiselle would like is a cup of weak tea and a slice of toast.'

Merry sat back on her heels and looked at me. 'I can try,' she said, 'but Mrs Deighton is all for cooking you a full cooked. At the very least she'll want you to have beef-tea. Reckons you'll need your strength to talk to the police.'

'Oh, are they here?'

'A local copper took statements last night, but Dr Simpson wouldn't let anyone see you, so they've sent someone over special this morning.'

'I'm honoured,' I said sourly.

'I was wondering if you'd like me to help you dress after breakfast?'

'Don't take the joke too far, Merry,' I said sitting up. Immediately the room rocked around

55

me. I pressed my hands against my head.

'Here, steady,' said Merry, jumping up to help me lay back down. 'I'll tell them you're not up to it. You're right white. Pally-wally, Rory said, or something like it.'

'No, I'd like to get it over with. If they stand any chance of getting the intruder then the earlier I tell them the little I know the better.'

'Be it on your head,' said Merry, frowning.

And so, after I'd managed to force a little break-fast between my lips and Merry had helped me into proper attire, there was a knock on the library door and in walked the police.

'Why, Sergeant Davies!' I said in astonishment. 'How nice to see you.' I blushed. 'I don't mean the circumstances are nice, but...'

'Miss St John.' The sergeant pulled up a chair and took out his notebook. He licked his pencil in preparation and took a deep breath. 'So, what's this I hear about you tangling with Bolsheviks again?'

'Bolsheviks? Good God,' I exclaimed with anger. 'Surely no one is trying to pass off that old line again!'

'Just my little joke, miss. Though it's interesting to see how you never believed the official line about the late Lord Stapleford's death. Endorsed by my inspector it was. But there you obviously know better, being an exceptionally bright young lady.'

I sank back into my pillow and tried to compose my thoughts. On our last encounter I had suspected Sergeant Davies of being perceptive, intelligent, cunning, but straight as a die. I saw no reason to change my opinion. 'I would hardly claim to know better than the police, sergeant,' I said politely. 'I'm very sorry if I gave you that impression.'

'Just tell me you 'aven't been hauling any dead bodies around by the leg this time?'

'I wasn't aware we had any dead bodies,' I said shortly. 'Oh no, is Mrs Wilson...?' I couldn't bring myself to finish the sentence.

'Not as far as I know, miss. Dr Simpson tells me it's touch and go. In the hands of the Lord, as they say.'

'Poor woman. I never liked her,' I said bluntly, 'but I'd not wish this on my worst enemy.' Something struck a chord in my mind, but it was fleeting and gone in a second. The sergeant was speaking.

'If the toffs – I mean, the ladies and gents – are to be believed nothing occurred during the séance except a little high spirits.' He laughed at his own joke and then suddenly stopped. 'But I was thinking 'ow it might all be connected. What do you think, Miss St John?'

'Mrs Wilson was certainly very upset at being included. She reacted badly to the messages.' I hesitated unsure of how much to say.

'Anything in particular?'

'One about a child not being wanted by its mother.'

Sergeant Davies blew out his moustache. His pencil hovered over the page. 'Now that sounds like a keg of powder if ever there was one.'

'Indeed,' I said.

'I want you to think carefully, Miss St John, do

you know anything about this delicate matter?'

'No,' I said slowly. 'I don't know anything.'

'But you've heard rumours and you have ideas?'

I decided it was time to change the subject. 'You're not a local man, are you, sergeant?'

'No, miss. I'm a Londoner. I married a young woman in service, much like yourself, and she came from this part of the world and had fancy to be near her family, so I transferred down.'

'I bet you regret that now.'

'Since I've had the pleasure of making your acquaintance I've been more and more inclined to that way of thinking.'

'So you never knew Mrs Wilson when she was young – and if there was ever a Mr Wilson?'

'I believe housekeepers are generally called Mrs unless they are ridiculously young, Miss St John.'

I grinned at the blow. 'Dr Simpson, the family doctor, told me once he'd known her from a young girl.'

'Did he, miss? That might be useful or this might turn out to be another of them Bolshevik cases again. Unless you can tell me anything about the attacker?' he asked hopefully.

'I can only tell you he was a little below average height, not heavily built, but still powerful. Wiry, I suppose. And that he had blue eyes.'

Sergeant Davies gave me a level look. 'Are you aware of how accurate a description that could be?' he asked.

'I don't follow you, sergeant.'

'Can I ask you to keep that description between ourselves for now?'

'Of course,' I said. 'Anything to help the police.'

'And might I have your word, miss, that you won't go blundering around in this case stirring things up.'

'I have no intention of blundering.'

'Good,' said the sergeant. 'Only this will be the third time you've been involved with murders around this family and that doesn't look good for anyone. People, and I'm not saying who, might start thinking you know more than you're saying. That you, in common parlance, know too much for your own good.'

Chapter Four

Mr Bertram Has an Idea

Despite Merry's roaring fire I found myself shivering. Sergeant Davies had shut up his notebook and departed leaving me with conflicting feelings. However, I was not destined to have the rest Dr Simpson had prescribed. The door had barely closed when it opened again to admit Mr Bertram. He had an expression on his face I couldn't read and moved into the room almost on tip-toe.

'I'm fine,' I said, half-lifting my head off my pillow and immediately regretting it. 'Or I will be.'

'Good. Good. I'm glad to hear it, Miss St John. You gave us all quite a shock.'

'Is there something wrong?' I asked. 'You're acting...' I broke off as I saw the reason for Mr

Bertram's behaviour had followed him into the room.

'Good heavens, Bertram. This must be the warmest room in the house,' said Beatrice Wilton. 'So interesting how people treat their servants.'

Mr Bertram blushed. 'I'm sure Miss St John is very grateful to Lord Stapleford for the care he has arranged.'

'Indeed, I am,' I said, gently sliding up my pillows. 'How may I help you? I'm afraid the doctor does not think I will be able to return to my full duties for several days.'

'So we heard,' said Miss Wilton, seating herself on the edge of a chair and sniffing slightly.

'Miss Wilton is a journalist,' said Mr Bertram. 'She writes the Lady Grey column.'

'Really, Bertram, there's no need to explain. I doubt the girl has ever read a newspaper in her life.' She leant forward, peering short-sightedly at my face. 'She is very young.'

I guessed there were very few years between us and I was sure that thanks to my father I was far better read than any gossip columnist, but it was hardly my place to say so. I smiled politely. Mr Bertram, who had cause to know that smile, rushed on.

'Miss Wilton has a journalist's mind. She may have some insights into the current situation.'

'Really, Bertram, you make it sound as if we're going to discuss the matter with the girl. You'll confuse her.' She turned with a smile, even more unfriendly than mine, towards me. Then she edged her chair slightly forward, blocking much of the heat from me. 'I want to ask you some questions, Ursula – isn't it?'

'Euphemia.'

She waved her hand dismissively. 'Don't worry, I will keep them simple. I only ask that you give me the facts, not your own ideas.'

Mr Bertram coughed. 'Actually, Beatrice, Euphemia has been most helpful in the past when there were, er, family difficulties–'

'Bertram, you asked me to help. Now trust me to do my job.'

'Of course, Beatrice.'

I looked from one to the other. Surely he couldn't have developed a soft spot for this terrible woman.

'Now, Euphemia, if you could tell me what you know about Mrs Wilson's affair?'

'I don't know anything about it.'

'So you do know that she had one?'

'No, I didn't say that,' I said.

'Euphemia worked here for less than a year,' said Mr Bertram.

'Hush, Bertie. You men never realise how much servants gossip. Now, Ursula, you can tell me the truth. I'm not here to judge.'

'But, ma'am,' I said carefully. 'You asked me only to tell you if I knew anything for a fact and I don't.'

'Oh, I see I was mistaken,' said Beatrice. 'You are much cleverer than I supposed.' To my horror she opened her purse and took out some coins. 'How much?'

'I am more than adequately compensated for my services,' I said coldly. 'As Mr Bertram said I worked at Stapleford Hall for a very short time.'

Beatrice Wilton leant forward and touched my arm. 'Come now, my dear, don't be proud. All servants can do with a little more than their masters give them. No matter how good they might be.' She laughed girlishly. 'I'm sure you do know something if you put your mind to it. Why, your Mr Bertram says you display almost to an educated standard.'

I shot Mr Bertram a furious look. To be fair, he did look embarrassed, but then to my astonishment he opened his mouth and said, 'If there is anything, Euphemia, you should tell Miss Wilton. She's a professional.'

'I'm tired,' I said, 'and I feel dizzy. I need to rest. I don't want your money, Miss Wilton. I don't know anything that can be of any help.'

Beatrice didn't budge an inch and her face took on an unbecoming mulish look. Sadly, she had her back to Bertram. I decided to up the stakes. 'In fact,' I said, 'I think I may vomit at any moment.'

'Good heavens!' said Bertram. 'We must leave at once. I shall send Merry to you.' He fairly bolted for the door. Miss Wilton gave me an astute look. 'I'm not as squeamish as Bertram,' she said, 'but I'll concede the field for now.' She got up and went to the door. She paused with her hand on the door handle. 'You may like to consider, my dear, that in a very short space of time your Mr Bertram and myself have found ourselves to be extremely compatible. Unlike Madam Arcana, I cannot foretell the future, but it may very well be in your best interests for us to reach agreement. I understand you have been invaluable in helping

Bertram,' she paused as though struggling for the right word, 'invaluable in helping Bertram sort things out.'

'He told you about that!' I gasped.

'Not everything, but he will. He seems uncommonly fond of you. Are you of him?'

'Your only interest is in filling your column,' I said astounded.

Miss Wilton raised one dainty eyebrow. 'I haven't decided what my interest is yet,' she said. 'But readers are always more interested in current news. One never needs to go raking through old material when one has new.' The accompanying smile was as lacking in warmth as it is possible for one alive to be. 'I'll leave you to your rest. We'll talk again later, I'm sure.'

I sat up and gaped at her, unable to find the words to express my shock. The smile widened and she left, closing the door gently and slowly behind her. I heard her calling for Bertram as she had intended I would. Her voice was sweet and low and, I feared Bertram would think, enticing.

The door had barely closed before Rory burst in. 'What's this? Are ye worse, lass? Do I need to send for yon doctor again?'

I settled my head back against the pillows. 'Do you realise you become alarmingly Scotch when you're upset?'

'Do I? It tends to slip out when I'm not concentrating. What's this about you being sick on Miss Wilton?'

'I wish,' I muttered under my breath. 'I'm fine, Rory. Or as fine as I was. She and Mr Bertram were pestering me with questions until my head span. I had to find a way to get them to leave.'

Rory came over and placed a hand on my brow. 'I wouldn't be surprised if they had worried you back into a fever,' he said angrily. 'I've half a mind...'

'Not to say something to our betters, Rory?' I said. 'That's not like you.'

'Aye, well. From what I've heard every time you've got mixed up with the Staplefords it's not come out good for anyone, but they can shrug it off. Look at me. I can't get a job anywhere else now I've been arrested for murder. Even that policeman was looking at me strange. I bet Stapleford's seen to it that the local nick has heard about my past association with the communists.'

'But you were cleared,' I protested.

'That's what I'm trying to tell you. Mud might slide off their groomed, greasy backs, but it sticks to ours.'

'I don't understand why he would do that.'

'Because he doesn't want to lose me.'

'Back-handed compliment?'

'And he doesn't want to pay me what I'm worth.'

'Oh,' I said, casting my eyes down. 'I'm sorry about all the stuff I got you involved with last time.'

'Nay, lassie. I wasn't for scolding you. If it hadn't been for your help I'd have ended my days swinging from a noose. I'll always be grateful for that.' He took a breath. 'Now, don't go biting my head off. It's just that I don't want to see that stuff happening to you. Leave 'em to it. Don't get involved this time. Mrs Wilson has been no friend to either of us and, while I'd not withhold information on what happened to her if I knew, I'm not going to be sticking my neck out to help. And I'd suggest you follow my lead.'

'Yes,' I said.

'Yes?' said Rory. 'Are you sure you're not feeling worse, Euphemia? You've never given in without a fight before.'

'Mr Bertram appears to have all the help he needs from Miss Wilton.'

Rory finally removed his hand from my head and sat down beside me. 'Och, lass, it was only time before he found someone of his own standing to help him with his mysterying.'

'That's not even a word.'

'You're jealous,' said Rory.

I blinked. 'I am not jealous,' I spluttered. 'Besides, he helped me.'

Rory shook his head. 'Green as the grass in the park.'

I ignored this. 'Much help she'll be. She practically offered me money to make up lies. She'll do anything to fill that column of hers.'

'It's not uncommon for the toffs to tip servants,' said Rory. 'Though it's uncommon for it to be an adequate tip.'

'You don't understand,' I said. 'She's evil. Nothing matters to her but the column. Mr Bertram is under her spell. She told me he had been telling her all the old family secrets – and the things he and I know, Rory, you'd not believe it! And she said that if I didn't help her with what was happening now, if I didn't give her some current dirt, she'd dig up all the old stuff about the late Lord

Stapleford. Mr Bertram doesn't understand – he's a lamb to the slaughter.'

'Now, Euphemia...'

'I am not making this up, Rory!'

'I never thought you were, lass. All I'm saying is stay out of it. It's as clear as the nose on your face that Beatrice Wilton is up to no good. My advice is: keep your mouth shut.'

'But Mr Bertram! He has no idea.'

'You're his housekeeper, not his guardian angel.'

'But I can't let him fall prey to this menace!'

'Euphemia, even if you have the audacity to tell him his new lady friend is a scheming hussy he'll never believe you.'

'Yes, he will! We've been through a lot together.'

'No, he won't,' said Rory gently. 'No matter how much this man favours you, you will always be a servant in his eyes and the word of a servant against a toff is never accepted. Especially when the toff in question is a very attractive young woman.'

'Is she?' I asked. 'I didn't notice.'

Rory grinned. 'You're no a male. Fine figure of a woman that. Pity, she's a scheming bitch from hell, but your Mr Bertram will have to find out in his own time.'

'But...'

'Has she dropped hints about having you fired yet?'

'Yes,' I said with fury. 'She has. She said if we didn't reach agreement she could make things ... well, she didn't say, but she implied.'

'And if you complain about her you'll play right

into her hands. Don't put the man in the position of choosing between you, Euphemia, because it won't be you he chooses.'

I remained silent.

'You know I'm right, don't you?'

I sighed. 'Yes. But what do I do?'

'Let them blunder around on their own. Your Mr Bertram's an impulsive sort. Without a calm, rational mind behind him he's not going to get anywhere.'

'But what if she makes good her threat?'

'She wouldn't dare. From what I've heard – and it's only rumours, mind – if my master didn't have friends in high places he'd not be where he is today.'

'But that's a point. He did...'

Rory put up his hand to shush me. 'Think about it, Euphemia. If my master can walk away from what he's rumoured to have walked away from, do you think he'd have difficulty squashing the column of a silly society gossip? The paper would never dare print anything against him.'

'You're right,' I said miserably. 'But that's not right either.'

'If you ask me nothing in their world is right. That's why we're well advised to leave it alone.'

'You really think if I do nothing this will all go away.'

Rory nodded. 'Trust me,' he said.

'You're about the only person I do.'

He grinned at that and dropped a swift kiss on my forehead. Then he blushed, muttered about his duties and left.

I was left alone for much of the day. Merry

stopped by with food and chattered with much excitement about the goings on. But as far as I could tell nothing had happened and no one knew more than they had last night. It must have been early evening, and I was dozing by the fire, enjoying what must have been the laziest day of my life, when Mr Bertram came to visit me alone.

'How are you, Euphemia?' he asked, offering me a glass. 'I thought a sherry might help.'

'Thank you,' I said, accepting what was obviously meant as a peace offering with as much grace as I could muster.

'I'm sorry about earlier,' said Mr Bertram. 'Beatrice is very passionate about her work.'

I nodded, remembering my discussion with Rory, and kept my mouth shut.

'It can take her to some shady places from what she's told me,' continued Mr Bertram. He was standing awkwardly, shifting slightly from foot to foot. 'I don't believe she is used to meeting servants of your calibre.'

'Not ones as well educated perhaps,' I said before I could help myself.

Mr Bertram sat down. 'I never said that. She misunderstood. I never described you as almost educated. I commented on your intelligence and, well, she took me up wrong.'

'It doesn't matter, sir,' I said politely.

'But it does. She feels terrible that you might feel insulted. She's such a sensitive soul. Amazingly so for the work she does. She says she has to positively steel herself to ask questions at times.'

'Poor lady,' I said barely managing not to choke

on my sherry.

Mr Bertram's face lit up. He had it badly. 'I knew you'd understand, Euphemia. You're very alike, the pair of you. Both independently minded, strong women. Of course, you're different stations, but if your life had been different I'm sure you would have made a fine journalist.'

I tried to take this as a compliment and smiled.

'You're not saying very much.'

'There isn't a lot for me to say, sir. I honestly don't know anything about Mrs Wilson's past. I saw the same as you that she was upset by the message and something Dr Simpson once said to me did make me wonder, but,' I shook my head, 'I don't know anything and I think in situations like this knowing is the important thing, isn't it? Whoever attacked her was very serious about it and I wouldn't want to mislead the police in any way with unfounded stories,' I said biting my lip.

Mr Bertram gave me a hard look. He knew exactly what I meant. 'It's been our experience, hasn't it, Euphemia, that the police aren't often up to the mark? Last time I tried to stop you interfering it put Rory's neck on the line. If you hadn't ignored me and gone your own way then he wouldn't be with us today.'

'That was an exceptional circumstance,' I said as levelly as I could. It was extremely trying to have one's own arguments used against one. 'Has anyone been accused for Mrs Wilson's attack?'

'The whole house is under suspicion. It's intolerable!'

'Not you or Rory. And surely not the ladies?'

'The figure was not especially tall and reasonably slight.'

'Which will let out your brother,' I said with a smile.

'I don't think the police are taking my description that seriously,' said Mr Bertram glumly. 'It's not as if any of us saw anything that was defining.'

'But...' I started then stopped. 'But you and Rory were up close with the man – person – didn't you see eye colour or hair colour or anything?'

'Sergeant Davies told me that no one could give him any particular details.'

I frowned.

'Do you know something, Euphemia?'

This was the point to tell Mr Bertram about seeing the assailant's eye colour; the clear opportunity to tell him about my conversation with Dr Simpson.

I struggled to find the words to tell him his own family doctor suspected his own father, who it's true he had had no cause to love, had fathered a child upon his own housekeeper.

'You see,' I began. I swallowed. For many reasons, not least our own unusual, if innocent, relationship, it was hard to find the words.

Mr Bertram edged forward. 'Yes, Euphemia?' Sergeant Davies and Rory's warnings rang in my mind. My impulse was to tell him the truth.

'You see...'

His eyes were alight with anticipation, waiting for me to crack the mystery or at least offer up the first clue. I hesitated. There was so much danger here, for all of us, and I was unsure how well he understood this.

'Should I get Miss Wilton? Is it something she

should know?'

I considered then saying my piece about his new friend. The good Lord knew Mr Bertram and I had argued many times, but always he had stood in my corner and I in his. But our unorthodox relationship had shifted with the arrival of Miss Wilton on the scene.

I made my decision.

'Euphemia, do you know something? You must tell me.'

'You see, sir, as I told Miss Wilton, I don't know anything at all.'

Chapter Five

London Bound

Mr Bertram sat back with a heavy sigh. 'I thought if anyone would have spotted anything it would have been you. I suppose Miss Wilton was right.'

'Right?'

'She said I was foolish to place so much expectation on your shoulders.'

I immediately had a strong impulse to confess not only what I knew, but everything I suspected, but my mother's training must have been better than she ever suspected. I held my tongue.

'I'm worried about staying on in the house,' said Mr Bertram. 'I don't like the risks. I was thinking of going away for a while.'

'Of course, sir, if that's what you need to do,' I

said coldly. I wasn't accustomed to considering Mr Bertram a coward.

'Miss Wilton's heart isn't equal to another shock so soon and your infamous tendency to meddle is doubtless putting you in danger.' Mr Bertram stood and began to pace. 'There is no other answer, I shall have to take you both away. Do you think you could act as a lady's chaperone, Euphemia? You're very young, but if I take you both it might quiet the gossips.'

I stared at him as if he had broken into another language. 'You cannot be serious, sir,' I finally managed to gasp.

'You're thinking it will look suspicious?' Mr Bertram turned to grin at me. 'I have thought this through. I shall tell the police where we are going, of course, but ensure they keep it in confidence. And I am very sure no one will guess our errand.'

The man was almost hugging himself with glee. 'Were you hurt in the attack, sir? Did he strike you also?'

Mr Bertram actually laughed. 'No, no, Euphemia. You're not the only one who can come up with a cunning plan. I've decided I shall help Miss Wilton with her next article.'

'Her gossip column?'

Mr Bertram laughed again. I had never heard him laugh so much so quickly. I began to be seriously worried. He sat down on the edge of the couch beside me and took my hand. 'I know I can trust you, so I'll explain. I'm sure Bea won't mind,' he stopped, 'well, she might mind, but once she's come to know you better it will be all right, so we'd better keep this between ourselves for now.'

I had the sense of moving out of my depth. Whatever Miss Wilton had told him I was categorically certain she did not intend him to repeat it to his favoured servant. Especially not his favoured female servant. Rory's warning had never struck me as more appropriate.

I struggled to sit up. 'Mr Bertram, you mustn't...'

'We're going to help Bea out with her very first piece of investigative journalism. You and me. With our keen brains and her writing ability we'll make her a star.'

'She's agreed to this?'

'Well, not yet, but I'm not as obtuse as you think, Euphemia. We've been chatting and I think she's not happy with her lot as a gossip columnist.'

'Oh,' I said. There didn't seem to be anything else to say.

'She mentioned she had a lead on something that would make a good story, but that she'd never be allowed to follow it. She said she didn't feel strong enough to – how did she put it – challenge the bastions of the male-dominated press alone. So I immediately thought we could help her.'

'And she likes the idea?'

'I haven't told her yet. She has no idea she set off this train of thought.'

'I see,' I said swallowing rapidly. 'She has no idea. She just happened to mention to a man she barely knows her secret, heart-cherished ambition.'

'I know,' said Bertram leaping to his feet. 'Isn't

73

it touching?'

'What exactly does she wish to investigate?'

'How we treat the mentally unbalanced in our asylums.'

'How opportune.'

'I don't think that's the word you mean, Euphemia. Opportune means–'

'Never mind, sir, you believe she will accept my help? I am a servant after all.'

'I thought we could start by telling her you'll be acting as a chaperone. I'll tell you what is happening and you can let me know your ideas. It will be quite like old times.'

I was lost for words.

'When the time is right I'll let her know how helpful you've been. I won't hog all the credit to myself, but if for a little while she thinks it's only me and it brings us closer – oh, Euphemia, you will help me, won't you?'

'I am your servant, sir, and hardly in a position to refuse.'

'Euphemia, when have I ever asked you to do anything you did not wish?'

At this point I realised that Mr Bertram was not, as I had hoped, immune to the delightful self-deception that servants were delighted to serve.

'Besides,' continued my smitten master, 'it's only an idea. She may not agree.'

'I'm certain she will accept your offer of help, sir,' I said unwisely.

'Thank you, Euphemia. You won't regret it. We will have a grand time.' And the besotted man burled from the room. I then did something I had never done in this house. I rang the servants' bell.

Within a very few minutes Merry was with me. 'Are you all right?' she asked breathless.

I lay back on my pillows, breathless and hot. 'I'm so sorry to ring for you, Merry, but I need to see Rory. It's an emergency.'

On reflection I could have chosen my words with more care. Rory arrived even more breathless than Merry had been and with a wild look in his eye. 'Euphemia!'

'I'm fine,' I said being even less careful with my words. After the very Scotch eruption had finished I explained my predicament with Bertram and Miss Wilton.

'Oh aye, I can see why that might be considered an emergency,' he finally admitted.

'But what do I do?'

'I take it your personal history would make it as difficult as mine to seek another situation.'

'I fear so,' I said grudgingly. 'I've never actually been accused of murder, but I'm aware that fingers have been pointed in my direction.'

'Aye, if you've come to general attention upstairs – and it has been mentioned elsewhere...'

'Miss Richenda,' I said sighing.

'I couldnae confirm or deny, but...'

'I need a wage for my family.'

'Then yer've no choice but to go along with it, but I'd recommend not seeing anything or offering any thoughts. Be as dumb as Beatrice Wilton thinks you even if it hurts your pride. This is a mess, Euphemia, and unlike Lady Grey I've nay doubt yer've a keen brain, but this is no tangle for the likes of us to untangle.'

He regarded me with an odd expression. I smiled. 'I'm not angry. You're right. But if I must go along with this, can I – can I rely on you?'

'Of course, lass.'

'I mean, if I do see things that–'

'It would be hard to keep tae yerself?'

'Yes and I won't be able to help putting it all together or trying to.'

'Making six out of four as usual,' said Rory with a grin.

'I'm out of my depth.'

'I'll be here for yer, lass. You can tell me anything.'

'And if you think I should go to the police?'

'I'll tell you, but if I'm honest I think you'll find a whole lot of speculation and possibilities and nothing strong enough to stand up in court. That's how it is with them upstairs.'

'I could try Mr Edward. He told me how to find him.'

'He did, did he?' said Rory. 'Fitzroy too?'

I shook my head.

'Well, that's something,' muttered Rory darkly. 'But honestly, lass, I doubt you'll come across something that affects the security of the nation.'

'With the Staplefords you can never be sure,' I said wearily.

'Aye, I'll gie yer that.'

We set out in Mr Bertram's motor in two days' time. Miss Wilton was keen to be gone and it took both Dr Simpson and Rory's combined efforts to delay the expedition for as long. As it was the world still had a slightly underwater feel to it. When I exited by the servants' door small, suitcase in hand, only to be told by Miss Wilton I was to be sitting in the Dickie seat I put my foot down. I was as polite as I was haughty and, by the time Bertram appeared on the scene, we were within moments of drawing hat pins and duelling. I wouldn't normally have considered Mr Bertram a quick-thinking man. He was certainly impulsive, but those impulses often seem to display a lack of intelligence rather than a surfeit. However, in this case he surprised me. 'But, ladies,' he said calmly, 'we are not taking my car. I've arranged to borrow one of Richard's. Merrit will drive it for us and Euphemia will sit up the front. Exactly where a lady's mai...' He encountered my eye. 'A lady's companion would sit.'

Waiting for us in a smart chauffeur's uniform was Merrit. 'I didn't know you could drive,' I said as he gallantly handed me into my seat.

'How hard can it be?' said Merrit.

I must have blanched, because he chuckled. 'Cheer up, Miss St John. We've got ourselves a nice jolly away from the house of doom.'

I glanced quickly behind us. There was a clear pane of glass in between. 'They can only hear us if they use the speaking tube,' said Merrit. 'It gives an illusion of privacy.'

'For whom?' I asked sharply.

'Both,' said Merrit. 'There's something I've been meaning to ask you, Miss St John and this seems like a good time. Oh, wait a minute, they are wanting to be off.'

I was glad to discover that Merrit could indeed

drive and we were soon smoothly underway.

'I've been thinking about my position and having some talk with Mr McLeod. He's ready to train me and I can see a number of benefits in transferring to Stapleford Hall.'

'Really?' I said. 'A number?' He had the grace to blush.

'But even if Lord Stapleford were happy to take me on as senior footman I wouldn't want to leave you and Mr Bertram in the lurch.'

'Oh, Merrit,' I said sadly. 'I'm really not the one to ask. So many things are up in the air right now.'

'Aye, and if our master were to take a wife, then maybe he'd want a butler? You'd not be adverse to a new maid in the household, would you, Miss St John?'

'Do you mean...?' I began. 'But you've only just met.'

'In our way of life, Miss St John, you don't tend to have long to make up your mind. We live by the will of them upstairs, so I reckon we have to grab the life we want when we can.'

'Is that what Mr McLeod said?'

'Aye, he was right direct about that. I wondered how he might have had a disappointment like. Though from what Merry tells me the younger staff are all mad for him, so he's bound to have his opportunities.'

'Indeed.'

'Have I said something to offend, Miss St John?'

'No, but we came very near to that tree. I think you'd be best to keep your concentration for the road.'

'But you'd put in a word with the master for Merry, would you, ma'am?'

'Of course,' I said peevishly. 'Merry is my oldest friend. I'll always do what I can to help. Though whether you're a good prospect for her or not I've yet to judge.'

This effectively rendered Merrit silent. It was at this point I realised that no one had told me where we were going and now I had no one to ask.

I can only place it down to the concussion, but I lapsed into a dream-like state for the rest of the journey. My eyes were open, but my mind was occupied with the strangest images. Lord Stapleford attacked by his own moustache during a dinner party with his late father and their equally deceased Cousin Georgie, both of whom were undoing their shirt collars and pleading for windows to be opened so they could cool down before they returned. Georgie asked me if I had seen his second-best trousers. Mrs Wilson chased a figure futilely into the distance, but fell into a giant bottle and lay there trapped like a giant fly, beating uselessly at the glass. Mrs Deighton made dish upon dish of meat for Rory, all of which he dropped at her feet. I intervened in this instance only to be told that dropping meat was the best way to meet a spouse. And all of this happened under a cloud of eyes. One pair was bright blue and sparkling and another of indeterminate hue, but I knew they belonged to Mr Fitzroy, who was carrying out his threat of watching the Staplefords. In the dream I sensed he was waiting for the house to fall about their ears so he could carry off any spare guns. I was in the process of explaining to Rory how if one walked between the beams one wouldn't fall through the floor, when I became aware of people speaking.

'Euphemia?' Bertram's voice.

'Miss St John?' Merrit.

'Oh really, Bertram, the girl is merely asleep. Let's get into the hotel. I am cold,' said Beatrice Wilton.

Slowly my surroundings came into focus. The street was full of noise and bustle. Tall buildings surrounded me and the air tasted of soot. We were in London. I was desperately cold and no longer had feeling in my extremities. My head pounded and I struggled to full wakefulness.

'I think I need to lie down,' I said through shivering lips.

'Of course,' said Bertram, hurrying round to help me from the carriage.

'Really, you need to escort me in!' said Miss Wilton peevishly. 'Not your servant.'

'Merrit has to station the car,' said Bertram in a low voice.

'This isn't suitable!' said Miss Wilton.

We began to mount some shallow steps. It took enormous effort and I had to concentrate on each pace forward. Without Mr Bertram's support I am sure I would have fallen.

'I shall tell the desk clerk she is a distant relative acting as your companion.'

'Bertram, you cannot do such a thing!'

'Beatrice, it was your journalistic zeal that dragged poor Euphemia from her sickbed.'

'The girl is malingering. She is enjoying every moment of this.'

I leant heavily on Mr Bertram's arm and did not enter the debate. In the end he escorted me to my chamber. I was not put in the servants' quarters, but the desk clerk had judged to a nicety my situation and Miss Wilton's disapproval. I was in one of the smaller rooms reserved for poor relatives of rich patrons. Compared to even my rooms at White Orchards it was pure luxury. Mr Bertram informed me he had left orders for my supper to be delivered to my room and I was not to think of anything but getting well until tomorrow. 'And if you feel worse at any point promise me you'll ring for the hotel doctor,' he said. 'I'll ask Bea to check in on you before she retires.' He shuffled awkwardly from foot to foot. 'It wouldn't be proper for me to... She is most concerned for your welfare.'

'Thank you,' I said, wishing he would leave so I could rest by the glowing fire.

'She is one of those ladies who does not find travel easy.'

'I see.'

'She didn't mean anything by... I'm sure when you know her better...'

'I'd very much like to lie down, sir.'

'Of course. Of course. If there is anything you should need the reception clerk has orders to supply you with ... well, anything. Please don't worry about the bill. I feel it was wrong of me to bring you when you are still so unwell. I didn't understand Dr Simpson fully. Beatrice assured me she had talked to him – you both being females –

and it was understood you were well enough to travel.'

It was clear nothing less than drastic action would move him and so I made my way across to the bed and began to untie the laces on my boots. Mr Bertram fled.

A good supper, a fine night's sleep and I was prepared to face them at breakfast in the morning. I had expected to eat in my room, but the clerk rang up to tell me I was expected downstairs. My head was clearing and I was looking forward to seeing Bea Wilton's face when she learned she was to sit at a table with me.

When I arrived she was midway through a lecture to Bertram. She did the only thing a lady could do under the circumstances of finding herself sitting alongside her potential fiancé's housekeeper and ignored me.

'Moral therapy began as far back as the 1790s,' she continued. 'It's quite fascinating and based around a lot of the Quaker thoughts. You know of them, of course?'

'Of course,' said Bertram, focusing intently on his boiled egg. He had yet to cap it and was showing all the nervousness of a man who was unsure if he would shortly be attempting to consume a running yolk in front of a lady he hoped to impress. In his shoes I would have ordered my eggs scrambled and did so to a passing waiter. He nodded, but also sniffed slightly displaying to a nicety his understanding of my station at this table. Bea broke off to beam at him.

'It's all about exercise and doing very routine and ordinary things. The hope is that those afflicted will be able to find a way in society in time.'

Bertram sliced off the top of one oval with such force he knocked the top onto the cloth. 'Good gad! You mean they let them out?'

Bea gave a trilling little laugh. 'Oh not the ones from the best families. They do tend to be the worst, don't they? I wonder why?'

I refrained from enlightening her.

'No, Bertram, the ordinary people, so they can be useful. Some of these institutions even have things for sale.'

'That anyone wants?' asked Bertram nobly trying to both ignore the mess he had made and signal the waiter.

Beatrice shrugged. 'I have no idea. What I do know is that for a long time visitors have been absolutely forbidden in these places. But everything is changing. Have you read any of the works by Dr Freud? Such strange ideas, but quite compelling.'

Bertram blanched. 'Beatrice, those are not suitable books for a woman!'

'I quite agree,' said Beatrice calmly nibbling on a slice of toast. 'But they are quite all right if I read them as a journalist. I don't know if he is an alienist exactly. He seems to suggest that we are all insane rather than specifically study the insane. Or maybe I have that wrong.'

'Alienism?' I ventured.

'The formal study of the criminally insane,' said Beatrice with a cold smile. She signalled to the waiter, who responded at once and Bertram's mess was taken away. There was an awkward pause.

'Does that mean all criminals are considered insane?' said Bertram at last.

Beatrice laughed again. 'Of course, darling, one would have to be insane to act criminally. Subjects of the empire should be proud to obey its laws.'

'That depends if they have enough to eat,' I muttered under my breath. Beatrice flashed me a look and I hid my face behind my coffee cup, but not before I saw the look of shock ripple across Bertram's face.

'Don't you agree, Bertie?' asked Beatrice.

'I had never considered it that way,' he said. He dabbed nervously at his mouth, waiting to see if I would step in, but I did not. 'So this asylum we are visiting today, does it have anything to do with Freud or alienists?'

'I daresay there might be an alienist there, but my interest is in what we classify within society as insane. I mean, one listens to doctors, but really it's us who decides who go into these institutions, isn't it? I'm sure you know what I mean, Bertram. Every now and then someone or something about someone crops up, even in the very best families, and it's so much easier to give them a nice home away from all the gossip that would otherwise go on. It's protecting them, really.'

My coffee cup clattered in my saucer. Beatrice turned to me and nodded slightly. Bertram on the other hand looked completely blank.

'Surely there must have been cases in a family as old as yours?'

'My family isn't very old,' said Bertram.

'But it's so very influential. Especially right now with those rotten Germans threatening to invade at any minute.'

Bertram coughed and straightened his shoulders. 'I don't believe there has been any formal announcement of invasion.'

'Oh, darling, one does not announce these things! They just happen. Besides if you've read that book, you'll know all about it. Every word is true.'

'I don't read novels,' said Bertram. 'Nor do I move in political circles. My family has nothing to do with international affairs.'

My breakfast lay before me, congealing. I was fascinated. I could not tell if Bertram was fascinated or repelled. But then Beatrice said something that made it clear, at least to me, that she knew nothing at all.

'One hears so much working in the newspaper industry.'

'Of course,' said Bertram. 'When is our appointment with Mr Freud?'

'Oh, darling, we're not seeing Freud. We're going to see a very nice, new asylum where no one is too mad. And I am going to write an entirely suitable piece on how we help those less fortunately minded than ourselves.'

Some time later I was waiting with Bertram on the hotel steps while Beatrice put on her hat. As we had been standing there some 20 minutes I could only conclude it was a most complicated hat. 'Might be interesting,' said Bertram suddenly. 'I mean, if she's right about how only the insane act outside the law. We might be able to talk to an alienist chappie about how to actually spot insanity.'

I sighed. 'I think people commit crimes for the most ordinary reasons,' I said. 'Love, envy, greed, hunger, the desire for power or even anger at perceived injustice.'

Bertram nodded. 'I know. But it's a nice idea that one could simply tell, isn't it? That whole business with Pa...'

'Ssssh!' I hissed. Beatrice had appeared at the top of the stairs.

'There you are, Euphemia. Didn't you hear me saying I was going to put on my hat? You really have no idea of your duties.'

Bertram took her arm and guided her into the waiting carriage. 'She is pretending to be your companion, not your maid,' he said.

'But I thought that was how she joined your household – as Richenda's maid?' Bea lowered her voice. 'That she came from a background none of you speak about.'

I felt myself flush with rage and embarrassment. I kept my head enough to know that defending myself would only open up questions I had no intention of answering and contented myself with imagining how very hard I could kick Beatrice in this confined carriage if she pushed me much further.

'No,' said Bertram shortly.

'No?' asked Beatrice again.

'No,' said Bertram with a heavy finality.

'Oh, I'm so relieved,' said Beatrice with smile. 'When I heard she was your housekeeper...'

Bertram made a snorting noise. Beatrice patted him on the arm. 'I'm not like the females with whom you are normally acquainted,' said Beatrice.

'I'm a journalist. I ask the questions others dare not.'

'It seems to me that being an acquaintance of yours might be a risky business,' said Bertram.

'Indeed,' said Beatrice. 'My acquaintances tremble, but my friends have nothing to fear.'

My mind boggled with the games this woman was playing. She had hinted that Mrs Wilson's love child might have been locked up in an asylum. Was she now suggesting that courtship would prevent her from revealing any unpleasant truths about the Staplefords? I only knew she had picked the wrong man for strategies. Bertram clearly had no idea what she was talking about.

The carriage clattered to a halt and we all climbed out. Bertram checked his pocketwatch. 'Are we on time?' he asked.

'Oh, darling, you didn't think I'd let them know we were coming, do you?'

And with that she swept up the path towards a large white house. Bertram and I were left staring after her in horror.

Chapter Six

Inside the Asylum

'Isn't she splendid?'

It was then I realised that I had been mistaken on two accounts. Firstly, the look on Bertram's face was one of positive astonishment rather than horror and I had, for some time now, been making too much of coincidence. I had, as others had often chastised me for in the past, allowed my personal feelings and prejudices to influence my judgement.

None of Beatrice Wilton's comments had anything to do with Mrs Wilson and the séance. Her designs were far more earthly. She was planning ahead to the commitment of Richard Stapleford so Bertram's status as head of the family would be assured. Even the desire to be a journalist – something I could grudgingly admire – was liable merely to be a substitute for entertainment until she found herself a husband. I suspected she was an heiress in her own right, but as my mother would have put it she smelled of "print" and "the shop". The mystery of Mrs Wilson's attack remained, but Beatrice Wilton's behaviour was all too easily explained. The Stapleford title might be new, and in my opinion of no great importance, but to Beatrice Wilton being able to add the word "Lady" before her name was the height of her ambition. Hence her ridiculous nom-de-plume: Lady Grey.

'I don't believe you need me here, sir,' I said to Bertram. 'I can offer no possible insights in how an asylum works or should work.'

'You underestimate yourself, Euphemia. Before you arrived at breakfast Beatrice informed me she had suspicions about this place.'

'Suspicions?' I asked.

'She felt she could not say more without prejudicing me, but keen observation is key!'

'Are you coming?' called Miss Wilton. She had

the door open, and while she didn't exactly have her foot wedged over the lintel the gentleman in front of her appeared large and intent on filling the frame.

Mr Bertram hurried over to help. It very quickly became clear that tours of the asylum were not available. Not even for a price. This time even Mr Bertram blushed at Miss Wilton's vulgarity. However, by dint of throwing around the nebulous power of the press we were finally conducted into a Dr Frank's office and told he would see us shortly. By this point I was in a blush of mortification from my toes to the crown of my head.

As the door closed behind our dour escort Miss Wilton settled herself in a chair and took off her gloves. 'I feel that went rather well.'

Mr Bertram muttered something incoherent and I walked over to study a print on the wall.

'Oh come, Bertram. This isn't a social call. The press have the right to be forceful to gain information that is in the public interest. We are the eyes and ears of the empire.'

'Yes, but, Miss Wilton – Beatrice – they are trying to accommodate us.'

'All signs of – well, at present I can say no more – but all signs would have been hidden.'

'Of course. Of course. Although if the staff are generally of the size of our escort then I doubt there will be anything that can be done about seeing beyond the limits they set.'

'I can ask questions, Bertram. Do not underrate the power of enquiry.'

'But can you be assured of the veracity of their answers?' I said without thinking.

'I will know,' said Miss Wilton grandly. 'And then I will be able to take matters further. You couldn't possibly understand.'

As there was nothing I could say in response without lowering myself to her standards I turned my attention back to the print. It was an aerial view of sorts that assumed the vantage point of above the property and yet able to see through the walls and roof. The grounds of the asylum were extensive. To my astonishment it appeared to resemble more of a country house than any hospital I had imagined. Littered among the grounds were various buildings containing long rows of accommodations for men and women as well as central buildings where it seemed from the whimsical drawings some sort of extended family life took place. The grounds were scattered with pretty outbuildings and sports fields.

Miss Wilton came up behind me. 'There is no lake,' she said. 'I had heard these places mimicked the great houses, but without a water feature...'

I looked at her in astonishment.

'My dear Beatrice, I hardly think a lake would be a suitable aspect for an asylum for the mentally unbalanced.'

Miss Wilton looked at Mr Bertram blankly.

'I did not imagine it would be so large,' I said, breaking the awkward moment.

'We are considered a very small facility,' said a man in the doorway. He was of slightly below average height, neatly dressed in a tweed country suit and wearing small round glasses. 'But then in London land is not always to be easily had.'

Miss Wilton whirled. 'You are Dr Frank? Is that

a German name? Always take them off-guard,' she hissed to Bertram and me.

'No,' said the doctor in impeccable English, 'but I am often asked the question. The issue of the collective paranoid mania surrounding the Germans and gripping the general populace I find quite fascinating. Of course, the press, such as your own paper, Miss Wilton, hardly help matters.'

Touché, I thought, warming to this little man.

'If you would be seated I shall see what I can do to help you.'

Miss Wilton introduced herself and Bertram formally. I was dismissed as a companion and left unnamed. She then reiterated her desire to tour the establishment.

Dr Frank shook his head. 'Impossible. These are not the days of the Bedlam asylum. We provide a sanctuary for our patients. We are an asylum from the world that has brought pressure so harshly to bear upon them. We are not a zoo.'

'How convenient for you,' said Miss Wilton. 'Who then watches the watchers?'

'The Lunacy Commissioners may visit at any time of day or night without appointment,' said Dr Frank. 'And they frequently do so.'

Miss Wilton appeared at a loss for words.

'You are aware of the 1890 Lunacy Act?' continued Dr Frank. 'It is extremely difficult for even a pauper to be admitted in these modern times.'

'But the country is full of asylums and their inmates!' protested Mr Bertram.

'Indeed,' said the doctor, 'a sad reflection of our time. But I assure you each person admitted goes

91

through a most rigorous admission procedure. There are no mistakes.'

'Are you telling me that in the history of asylums that no unwanted members of rich families have ever been placed in the care of a place such as this?' asked Miss Wilton.

'One might say that all the people here are un-wanted members of the human family, Miss Wilton.'

'That is not what I meant!'

'I know, and I wish I could answer otherwise, but it is true that the evolution of the asylum has gone through more than one unfortunate phase.'

'So it is true!'

'I can assure you that no modern asylum har-bours anyone who should not be there.'

'But if someone was erroneously admitted before 1890 they would not now, after 26 years, be fit to re-enter normal life,' I said.

All heads turned towards me and Miss Wilton positively scowled.

'You are quite right, Miss, er...'

'St John.'

'Miss St John. You're not related to the St Johns of Lower Warmington, are you? A most interest-ing family.'

'Would anyone confess to be associated to a family of interest to an alienist?' I countered.

Behind his glasses Dr Frank's eyes twinkled. 'Well said, my dear. You are quite right. Long-term institutionalisation will rob even the sanest individual of the ability to live in the outside world. The world of the asylum is small and its morality comfortingly black and white.'

'So those who spend much of their lives within its walls are changed?' I asked.

Dr Frank now openly smiled. 'You are referring to the staff, I take it? How refreshing to encounter such a lively mind. Are you also with the press?'

'No, she is not,' snapped Beatrice. 'Answer the question.'

Dr Frank's good humour vanished. 'I would rather say that those of us who have witnessed the depressing deterioration of the human spirit under adversity or through the cruelties of nature have a different and perhaps more generous appreciation of the human race.' He frowned again. 'We care very much about those in our charge. Far more so than those who placed them here.'

'And yet being an alienist must set you apart and even give cause for you to see your charges as subjects for study?' I asked. 'My father was strong in the belief that family and church should care for the mentally afflicted rather than placing them in the care of strangers.'

Mr Bertram gave me an odd look.

Dr Frank nodded. 'There is much in what your father says. But at the heart of the matter is the mentally well do not wish to care for the mentally unwell. They fear illnesses of the mind as if they were infectious.'

'They're not, are they?' said Bertram looking alarmed.

Dr Frank shook his head. 'Not in the sense you mean.' He turned his attention to me once more. 'I assure you, Miss St John, I run this asylum on principles your father would approve of. We treat our inmates as if they were part of a large family.

We run orderly days with regular activities. We hold sports events and they enjoy light work. There is a great deal of satisfaction and sanity to be found in feeling useful and proud of oneself.'

'You are a most modern institution,' I said. 'Do you effect many cures?'

'A few,' said Dr Frank. 'Not as many as I would wish and generally of the mental illnesses that are caused by life events, such as the birth of a child. The deeper-seated illnesses are less likely to lift. Although we work hard to lighten our patients' burdens.'

'It all sounds quite admirable,' said Mr Bertram sincerely.

'What about the man who showed us in?' said Miss Wilton. 'He did not have the look of a gentle carer.'

Dr Frank sighed. 'This is an asylum. There is always the possibility of violent behaviour when the mind is overset. Yet one more reason why visitors are not permitted. For their own safety.'

'If I wished to have a family member committed?' asked Miss Wilton suddenly.

'You would need to provide a signed statement of social and medical history along with two detailed medical statements confirming the individual was an insane person or an idiot of unsound mind.'

'That hardly sounds difficult,' said Miss Wilton.

'The Lunacy Commissioners are able to release any patient if on two visits of more than seven days apart they are convinced of their mental health,' said Dr Frank coldly. 'The system is not open to abuse.'

Miss Wilton rose. She had sensed, as had I, that Dr Frank's patience was exhausted. 'In my world you would be surprised, doctor, what money can buy.'

And with this she swept from the room. Bertram muttered what could have been an apology and followed her.

'I'm very sorry,' I said to the doctor. 'She is...' I trailed off unable to make an adequate excuse.

'She is disappointed and frustrated,' said Dr Frank. 'Intelligence is the curse of women in our times. Be careful, my dear. You have more than your fair share.'

I shook hands and followed my companions. We were all shown out by a small woman in a neat apron who smiled and said how nice it was to have visitors.

'Is she?' said Bertram urgently in my ear.

'She's wearing a nurse's watch,' I responded, but I could understand why he had made the mistake. There was something too bright, too cheery in her manner. I could only imagine that such a bearing came of being daily positive in the face of human suffering.

The final door was opened by our original gate-keeper. He was as large and looming as my initial impression. One of his ears was broken into what I believe is commonly referred to as a cauliflower and his nose was askew. He stood close to the open door and, despite myself, I shrank back slightly. I was startled to see his lips curve up-wards. He was enjoying dominating us by his presence.

Mr Bertram rose to the occasion and slipped

him a coin. Then he ushered us out as casually as if we were all leaving a tearoom. It was quite the best response.

'What an awful place,' he said when we were safely back in the carriage. 'Dr Frank clearly does his best, but the atmosphere! You were very brave, Beatrice.'

'Yes, I was,' said Beatrice pulling at her gloves. 'Not that I accomplished much. There is a story there, but I have not yet made up my mind how to get at it.'

'You're not thinking of going back?' asked Bertram in alarm.

'No, but I think I might try and get an interview with one of those Lunacy Commissioners. Do you think they exist? Or was he fobbing us off?'

'I don't understand,' I said. 'I thought this topic had been the subject of investigation for you for some time?'

'It has.'

'But didn't you do any research?'

Beatrice Wilton's lips almost disappeared her smile was so thin. 'And what would you suggest?'

'Don't newspapers have cuttings libraries? Or even libraries.'

'How very interesting to meet a housekeeper who is so well informed. Perhaps you would like to tell me what my next step should be.'

'Well, I think,' I began without thinking. Beatrice interrupted me with a high, tittering laugh, 'Really, Bertram, this girl is too much. You must school your servants better! And, Ursula, please do not presume to tell me my job. A journalist must follow her instincts. A good nose, as we say in the

96

industry, is the best form of attack.'

I felt my eyebrows shoot up and my tongue longed to comment, but I caught sight of Bertram's face. 'I'm sorry, if I gave offence,' I said as politely as I could manage, though the words nearly choked me. 'I merely wish to be of assistance.'

My gracious apology earned me a curt nod. For the rest of the journey she conversed with Bertram in a low voice. My help was clearly not needed. When we arrived at the hotel Miss Wilton turned to me. 'You may have the rest of the afternoon off. Your presence is not required until dinner. Sadly, etiquette decrees I must not dine alone with Mr Stapleford, no matter how much of a gentleman he may be.'

I looked past her at Bertram, who was staring at his shoes. 'Sir?' I asked.

'You and Merrit could take this opportunity to fraternise. This is London, after all, and neither of you are needed,' said Beatrice.

'Fraternise?' I asked, assuming one of my mother's minor expressions of haughtiness.

I thought it had done the trick for the woman had the grace to blush. But she was made of stronger stuff. 'I'm sure it is very difficult for you to maintain the same level of decorum as Mr Stapleford and myself. I assumed you would relish the opportunity to spend time with someone of your own class.'

Merrit! My own class! My eyes were blazing so hard I could almost feel the heat. 'I take my orders from Mr Stapleford, miss,' I said in a low, level voice, which if she had known me better would have had her running for the hills.

Bertram snapped back to the present. 'I shall escort Miss Wilton upstairs. If you could wait for me in one of the smaller salons, I would be grateful for a word.'

I nodded. At last he was coming to his senses. However, when he finally joined me in the overly pink and frilly room, so not what one would expect in a modern establishment, his expression was one of fury.

'What the hell do you think you're up to, Euphemia? Miss Wilton is deeply distressed over your behaviour. She has had to go and lie down. I have sent for the doctor. She has a weak heart, you know!'

I stammered for a moment trying to find words to express my feeling of injustice.

'How dare you try to tell her how to perform her profession!'

'But it doesn't make sense,' I finally exploded. 'She knew nothing about the Lunacy Act. If she was investigating how the mentally ill are treated surely she would have some idea how the asylum worked?'

'She explained that! She said she needed to make Dr Frank think she knew nothing so she could catch him out.'

'Catch him out at what?'

'I don't know,' said Bertram. 'I'm not a journalist.'

'She was asking questions about how one might get a family member committed.'

'Yes, she was. That must be it. That must be what she suspects.'

'You don't think she might have had someone in mind?'

'No,' said Bertram. 'There is no insanity in her family. She has assured me of that.'

'That wasn't what I meant.'

'Then I don't follow you, Euphemia.' Bertram straightened his shoulders and curled his lip. His whole attitude was one of challenge.

I will always wonder if I had spoken then if things might have been different, but Rory's warning played in my mind. I also knew of no manner possible in which I could convince him that Miss Wilton, for all her riches, was in her own way a gold-digger and Bertram was the prize. As it was I took refuge in half-truths. 'I'm sorry,' I said. 'I'm very concerned over Mrs Wilson. She and I have never been the best of friends, but with her in hospital so ill and us so far away not knowing how she is faring...' I swallowed hard. 'I apologise if I have distressed Miss Wilton. I am not myself.'

Bertram read my bright eyes as being on the verge of tears instead of the anger and disappointment I was suppressing. His face lit up. 'Of course,' he said. 'I sometimes forget you are only a woman and do not have the male strength of mind.' He added quickly. 'I mean that as a compliment. You are the most capable young woman of my acquaintance, but you are still ill and shocked from the attack that terrible night.'

'My head does hurt and I am more than usually fatigued,' I said honestly.

'I should have told you earlier. I rang up Stapleford and I have reports that Mrs Wilson is doing as well as can be expected. She is not yet fully

99

conscious, but there is a policeman on hand to take her statement as soon as she recovers.' He paused. 'I must say I was quite impressed with the efficiency of that.'

'They may be concerned that her attacker will not wish her to regain consciousness,' I said.

'What a horrible thought!'

'But a very realistic one,' I said sadly.

Bertram pondered for a moment then exclaimed, 'But that means that you also could be in danger!'

'Possibly, though I have made it clear to the police I did not see the attacker clearly.'

'At least few people know where you are.'

'Only those at Stapleford Hall,' I replied.

An uncomfortable silence fell between us. Eventually Bertram said, 'I must return to see how Miss Wilton fares.'

'Will you need me?'

'No, the lady will be taking her dinner, if she can manage anything, in her room, so your escort will not be required tonight.'

'People might think her companion should attend her?' I ventured, though the last thing I wanted to do was spend time with someone I felt was both devious and malingering.

'I don't think that would be wise,' said Bertram. 'She needs rest, but I appreciate the offer. Why don't you go out and see a little of London for yourself? It's early yet and while a lady could never walk the streets alone I believe many London servants do.'

I smiled and nodded, though his speech daunted me in more than one way. I had no inclination to spend the rest of the day shut up in my room and I did not think the hotel would look kindly on a mere companion sitting alone in the lounging areas. I was dressed too simply. But the thought of wandering through London alone was too daunting. I stood hesitating when my eye caught the attention of the concierge, who smiled encouragingly. He was a tall, wiry chap dressed in a uniform with enough gold material to suggest his importance and not enough that he could be mistaken for a bellboy, who for some reason were inordinately flash. He was also considerably older than me. I walked up to his desk.

'Good evening, miss,' he said in a rumbling voice. 'How can I be of service?'

'It seems,' I said awkwardly, 'that my services as companion are not required for the rest of the day and my ma-mistress has suggested I take in the London sights. However, I confess I am alarmed at venturing out alone.'

The concierge grinned. 'Quite how it should be, miss. It's all very well for those maids to go racketing about unescorted, but for a lady such as yourself it's quite a different matter. You're with Miss Wilton, are you not?'

'Yes, I am,' I said startled at this man's perspicacity.

'A very nice young woman, I'm sure, but new money, I would imagine, and not quite up to how things should be done.'

'Is there something you could suggest I might do to fill my time?' I asked growing increasingly embarrassed.

'There is one of them spiritualists giving a talk

101

in the blue saloon,' said my new friend. 'There's a small charge, but we haven't sold many tickets, so I'm sure I could sneak you in. Being as how you are a resident.'

'Oh, I see. I'm not sure.'

'Let me check my list. It's a Madam Arcana.'

My heart skipped a beat. Coincidences do happen in life, but I am always wary of them. 'Yes,' I heard myself saying as if my voice came from a long way away. 'I have heard of her. It would be most interesting.'

'We'd better be quick then. Come with me, miss.'

He led me down a labyrinth of corridors, some of which I felt certain were servants' passageways. Finally, he ushered me through a side door with an entreaty to 'Enjoy myself.'

I found myself in a larger saloon than I had expected. It had a large, cavernous feel that was cold and unwelcoming. It was blue and it was filled with rows of corn-coloured chairs. These had been placed in rows facing a dais on which a familiar figure in a purple turban sat. The room was less than half full. I made my way down the aisle as quietly as possible and joined the last row of filled seats.

'Oh-oh-oh,' moaned Madam Arcana, who was either about to enter a trance or had severe food poisoning. I took the opportunity to appraise the audience. There were a number of girls dressed in plain, respectable dresses and which I guessed to be maids on their day out. There were also a goodly number of shabby-genteel women, who I took to be companions. In the front three rows I could see nothing but large feathered hats and these I took to be worn by older matrons, who formed the backbone of Madam Arcana's moneyed following. Standing, trembling near the centre was a woman in her early 20s, whose smart but threadbare skirt and jacket, sensible haircut and face devoid of makeup clearly marked her as a vicar's wife. I imagined her winning the egg-and-spoon race and tumbling along happily in the mothers' sack event.

'The Reverend Dipton says the church roof is more important than the refurbishment of the library,' proclaimed Madam Arcana suddenly. 'He says the fete should be used to raise money to shelter the faithful of God.'

'Are you sure?' said the woman in a nervous voice. 'Only my husband is quite clear that the roof will last another winter and the children are so short of books.'

Madam Arcana opened her eyes. 'My dear,' she said, 'I could not comment on the wisdom of the particular spirit you asked me to contact, but only pass on what he said.'

'You mean,' said the questioner in a startled voice, 'that he might be wrong? I thought on the other side...'

'Has he long been passed?' asked Madam Arcana.

'Some six months. Three months before my husband took the parish.'

'And was he revered as a wise and good man when he was there?'

'I really couldn't say,' said the woman in a tone that implied she very well could.

'He may still be adjusting to the higher vibrations,' said Madam Arcana. 'It can take some spirits time to throw off their worldly desires.'

'You mean we could do as we wanted?'

'Was there ever any reason why you shouldn't?'

The woman twisted a handkerchief between her fingers. 'The vicarage is so very dark and gloomy. It feels as if he is still there.'

'Then I strongly advise you to have a very happy and busy fete,' said Madam Arcana. 'He will see you are looking after his parishioners well and their jollity will extinguish his solemnity.'

'You mean, like a party?' asked the woman brightening. 'Oh, what a jolly idea.' She sat down very well pleased with what her shilling or whatever the entrance fee had cost her. I could only imagine the scene when she tried to explain her reasoning to her husband or perhaps she would have more sense.

'Does anyone else have a query?' asked Madam Arcana.

There followed a number of questions about lost dogs, lost wallets, who daughters should marry and the likelihood of an invasion by Germany. I was not once convinced that Madam Arcana was in contact with any spirits, but the dearly departed's – or rather *her* – advice was always gentle, sensible and inclined to make the questioner think for themselves. I almost approved. I could not say whether it was her deception or the inability of those present to listen to plain, common sense unless it was couched in the mantel of the day that dismayed me more. But then, as my father used to say, there is nothing common about common sense.

When the final question had been asked Madam Arcana indicated the tea trolleys that had been placed in the aisles. (I had been too wrapped up in her performance to notice their arrival.)

'Dear ladies and gentleman,' she nodded at the one young man in the audience, 'do help yourselves to refreshment. It is all included in your ticket price and after a session such as this we all need to replenish our energies. I will join, but,' she raised a finger and smiled, 'no more questions for our spirit friends. On general topics I will be happy to converse.'

There was a murmur then a round of applause. With almost undignified haste seats were pushed back as people made a beeline for the cake. I had intended to sneak away, but a particularly fine macaroon drew my attention and reminded me I had not had any lunch. Besides, there was clearly more than ample cakes unless they all proved to have appetites like the young vicar's wife. In the time I had hesitated she had polished off two slices of Victoria sponge and an iced biscuit.

'You should certainly help yourself,' said Madam Arcana appearing at my shoulder. 'George, the concierge, had strict instructions to ensure you attended.'

'From whom?' I asked.

'Why, me,' said Madam Arcana. 'I wanted to ensure you remembered my warning.'

'Beware for my enemies,' I said coldly. 'I take it you are referring to Mrs Wilson's unfortunate experience. I am surprised news has reached London so quickly.'

Madam Arcana smiled. 'I hear many things from many sources. But what I wished to remind you was that the message referred to enemies in the plural.'

'But I don't have any other enemies,' I said. 'Besides, we weren't exactly enemies, I merely disliked her greatly...' My voice trailed off.

'Excuse me, I have to check on someone,' I said.

Madam Arcana handed me the macaroon. 'Take this. You look as if you need it.'

Automatically, I took the confectionary she held out to me, so I was still grasping it in my hand when I arrived breathless and flushed, after several wrong turns, in the main entrance. I turned about me wildly and headed towards the main staircase. On it, descending, I met Bertram, his face streaming with tears.

'Oh, Euphemia,' he said. 'She's dead.'

Chapter Seven

Visiting Mr Edward

Poor Mrs Wilson. A wave of guilt swept over me. I had on more than one occasion wished she did not exist in my life, but I hoped I had never wished her dead. And in such a way.

'Euphemia, did you hear what I said? She's dead?' Bertram's voice broke. His face was as forlorn as Little Joe's had been when his first pet died. Bertram was still two steps above me on the staircase leaving me with a dilemma. I could hardly approach and comfort him. I certainly couldn't push past him and, even if he had the remaining sense to follow me downstairs, we could hardly conclude this conversation in a public place.

'I'm very sorry,' I said. 'Perhaps we should...' I attempted to indicate that we should return upstairs to our rooms.

'But what do I do?'

'I imagine the right thing to do would be to return home at once.'

'But she's up there...' He faltered and looked up the stairs.

'Dear God!' I exclaimed. 'You can't...You don't mean Miss Wilton! I thought you meant Mrs Wilson.'

'Why would I care about that old harridan?' said Bertram with more truth than charity. 'My poor Beatrice. It has all been too much for her. I found her just now lying in her boudoir no longer breathing.'

'Has a doctor been sent for?' I asked.

Bertram shook his head. 'She's dead.'

'It is not always that simple to tell if life is extinguished.' I turned and ran down the stairs to the concierge.

''Allo, miss. Did you enjoy the show?'

'George, something terrible has happened,' I said in a low voice. 'My – the honourable Mr Bertram Stapleford has this moment found Miss Wilton unmoving in her suite. He fears she is dead. Can you send for a doctor at once?'

George's eyes flashed me a look of sharp intelligence. 'I should be able to do better than that, miss. The doctor what she sent for is on his way.'

'The doctor what she – that *she* sent for?' I turned to Bertram, who was now standing behind me. 'I thought the doctor had already visited her.'

'That's what she said,' answered Bertram.

'Our man's a Dr Smith. Right good 'un, but very busy. If I'd realised it was so urgent I'd have chased him up.' The concierge looked quite dismayed.

'She had a weak heart,' I explained.

'It could have happened any time,' said Bertram. 'It's one of the reasons she lived her life as she did. Running at it. She always knew she might not have enough...' He swallowed noisily.

'Why that's tragic, sir. Why don't I find you a nice quiet corner and a large glass of something? We'll get that doctor here toutey sweet. Maybe the young lady's right – maybe it's only a deep sleep or coma sort of a thing.'

He ushered Bertram away, calling to a bellboy to round up Dr Smith and left me waiting at the desk. He was back a few moments later.

'Would you be willing to come up to her room with me, miss?'

'Of course,' I said. Though my father had tried to shield me of necessity I had come into contact with more than one corpse as a vicar's daughter. And since becoming part of the Stapleford household it would be somewhat of a relief to encounter a natural death.

'It's not like I think there's anything strange

going on, but in these circumstances we 'ave procedures to follow. I should ask the duty manager, but he's on his break.'

'Procedures?' I asked alarmed.

'I need to lock the door. Many of our visitors have travelled widely and there's some nasty things they've brought back. 'Ad she been abroad lately?'

'No, I don't think so. Do many people die in the hotel?'

'All the time,' said the concierge with a twinkle. 'Place is only slightly less dangerous than a hospital.'

'What? Oh, I see what you mean. People only go to hospital when they're sick. But the guests?'

'Often old ladies, retired gents, and those that 'ave picked up something nasty. Sheer numbers of people what come through here there's bound to be a dead body every now and then.' He stopped outside her door. ''Ere, you weren't close to this young lady, were you, miss? Only I didn't get that impression. I'm usually good at reading people, but you know no matter how many times it happens on your watch it rattles you a bit. I 'ope I 'aven't been inappropriate, like?'

I shook my head. 'We were not friends. I would not have wished her dead, but I can't say I am in any way as distressed as Mr Stapleford.'

'Aye, I can see he had a right fancy for her. But as they say what's for ye won't go by ye.' He slipped the key into the lock. It didn't turn. 'Seems like the poor young lady did my job for me before she died.' He shrugged. 'There's many can only rest behind a locked door.'

'But shouldn't we check if she is still alive?'

'Do you have any medical training, miss?'

'No,' I said and only just stopped myself from saying, *but I have considerable experience with dead bodies.*

'Then I doubt there is anything you could do for the lady.'

'But what if she's dying! Alone?'

'Mr Stapleford has reported her dead,' said George. 'That's good enough for me.'

'Let me go in,' I urged. 'Just to be sure.'

George squared up to me. 'No, we don't know what she died of. You're not sure if she's been abroad and I'm betting you have no idea if she's been in contact with someone who has, so I'm putting me foot down. It's a tragedy, but your death would only back it doubly so.'

'I'm sure you're exaggerating,' I said.

'Oh, the tales I could tell you. You'd shiver your skin right off your bones.'

'But she had a weak heart.'

'All the more likely to make her succumb to disease.'

Short of wrestling the key from him by force, and I had no expectation of winning such a battle, there was nothing to be done. I made my way back down to the saloon and Bertram.

''Course, if she is dead,' said George, 'we will 'ave to call in the police. But we'll keep it as quiet as we can for both your sakes and the hotel's.'

My heart sunk down into my boots. Yet again Bertram's name and mine would be connected with sudden death. It would be a wonder if we weren't carted away by the police on the spot.

110

However, I knew that any plea on my behalf to circumvent procedure would only bring suspicion down on both our heads, so I nodded, took a deep breath and went in to comfort Bertram.

He was not as I feared inebriated. The decanter George had generously provided stood untouched on the small table before him. In his hand he held a glass, but it was barely lower than a full measure. He looked up at me with the blank, startled stare I had seen on all too many faces of those recently bereaved in my father's parish. My heart stung. He must have cared deeply for her despite the short time they had had together.

'She said the doctor had been,' he said. 'She said he told her to rest and she would be fine. I'd never have left her alone if...' He struggled to continue.

I patted his arm awkwardly. 'No doubt she was trying to reassure you. She didn't want you to worry.'

'But it doesn't make sense. She didn't lie. She never lied to me.'

Now was not the time to assert my suspicions over Beatrice's motivations, but I could not resist saying, 'You were deep in one another's confidence, weren't you?' I tried to make it sound comforting, but I knew I was taking advantage.

'She told me everything,' said Bertram, finally taking a swig of his drink. 'I could, of course, never return the compliment. What you and I know, Euphemia. I had to keep her at arm's length... With a family like mine, I couldn't take advantage of her innocence.'

'You mean... Oh dear God, this changes everything. I've been so stupid.'

'Changes what?'

I considered for a moment. Was now the right time to raise my suspicions after all? It might make Bertram think a little less of me, but it would divert him. Only such a short acquaintance I strongly doubted that they had been in love. Although Bertram ever one to leap into situations with passion and lack of thought might well fancy it was so. It might also lead him into a devastating expression of grief. I took a deep breath. 'I thought you might have told her about your brother. From the questions she asked I thought perhaps you might be considering attempting to get him committed. Before he did any more harm,' I added.

'Do you think I'm a fool, Euphemia? Even if Beatrice was no more than a gossip columnist with aspirations she would be unable to let such a story pass her by regardless of her personal feelings. Print was in her blood.'

'But she hinted to me that she knew.'

'Of course she hinted. Journalists always hint they know more than they do. It's remarkably effective at getting people to be indiscreet.'

'Oh,' I said. When he was in one of his passions it was easy for me to forget that Bertram knew far more of the world than I, but every now and then he would remind me to shocking effect. On the positive side Bertram was now looking a lot more alert. He put his glass down.

'But her questions at the asylum. It was as if she was trying to provoke them.'

'I don't know the whole story. She only told me that she had strong suspicions and would feel safer with me around while she investigated.'

'Did she make notes?'

'Of course she did! Well done, Euphemia! They'll be in her room.' He stood up.

'Her room is locked.'

'But I have a key,' said Bertram pulling it from his pocket with a flourish.

'Put that away,' I said harshly, pulling down his arm.

'I suppose it does give the wrong impression,' said Bertram. 'But Beatrice had an abnormal horror of hotel fires. She only locked her room when she retired. She wanted me to have a key in case anything happened. Made me promise I'd rescue her.' He swallowed and reached for his glass.

A chill swept over me. 'But her room was locked,' I said. 'She would lock it if she was resting, wouldn't she?'

'No,' said Bertram. 'Only when she retired for the night.'

'The other doctor,' I began.

'You think there was one?' said Bertram.

'I am beginning to fear so.'

'Good gad! I can't believe it. I know we've had some extraordinary experiences, but not every death has to be murder, Euphemia. Some people do die natural deaths.'

Bertram handed me his glass and I took a sip of the fiery liquid. I choked slightly. 'We have had more than our share of bad luck,' I said.

'I'm rather afraid the police will agree with you.'

We sat in silence for a few minutes. 'I should contact her family,' said Bertram finally. 'I don't know what I will say to them.'

'I should ask to speak to her father,' I said. 'Her mother would be too distressed. They know of her heart condition, so although they will be naturally grief-stricken it will not be entirely unexpected.'

'What about our suspicions?'

'I wouldn't mention anything until we know.'

Bertram paled. 'And the arrangements?'

'Her family will want to take charge.'

'I shall offer any assistance in my power,' said Bertram.

'Of course.'

His face fell. 'But I have no idea of what I can do.'

I took a large swallow of Bertram's drink, handed him back the glass and stood up, 'But I do. I'm going to see Mr Edward.'

'What?'

'He gave me a contact address in London in case I ever needed it.'

'But, Euphemia, this is hardly security of the realm stuff!'

'I don't know what it is. But his words were if anything untoward begins again at Stapleford Hall they would be keen to be made aware.'

'But Beatrice's death has nothing to do with Mrs Wilson's attack.'

'Doesn't it?'

'How could it?'

'I don't know, but I have a feeling.'

'Euphemia, you can't go to that man with a

feeling! Do you realise how important he is?'

'I don't know what he is,' I admitted. 'But I think we need his help.'

We argued for a while, but the concierge came back to say the doctor had arrived and they were now having a discussion as to whether the room should be opened before the police arrived. The doctor thought it should and George disagreed. 'My manager is still on his break, sir. So it's a bit of an awkward one. I thought you might be the best person to sort this out?'

Reluctantly Bertram went off with him. His parting shot to me was, 'And don't go anywhere, Euphemia!'

Of course I waited for them to clear the stairs before heading to my room and fetching my coat.

I gave the address Mr Edward had given me to the cabbie and was surprised when in a very short time we pulled up outside a large building. It seemed to be comprised of offices and apartments and did not in any way look like a government building. I climbed the dingy staircase feeling more and more as if someone was playing an enormous joke on me. When I arrived at the right floor the door in front of me bore the legend of a private detective agency. Had Mr Edward changed jobs? However, I had come this far. I knocked on the door and went in.

A smart young woman was sitting at a desk. She looked up brightly and smiled. 'How can I help?'

'I fear I may be in the wrong place,' I said. 'I was looking for Mr Edward.'

'And you are?'

I hesitated a moment and then gave my real name. Fitzroy had indicated he knew it and I was fairly certain what he knew Mr Edward would also know. The young woman gave me another bright smile and reached into her desk. She brought out a clipboard and traced her finger down a list of names. 'Ah, here you are. Is this a matter of urgency?'

'To be perfectly honest I don't know. There has been one serious attack, possibly a potential murder, and another young woman died today, but that may have been due to natural causes.'

'Were any of these persons of significance?'

I repressed the urge to retort that all human life was of significance. 'One was the housekeeper at Stapleford Hall, the home of the Staplefords, and the other a daughter of the Wilton press family.'

The young woman nodded. 'I think that will suffice,' she said. 'If you will follow me.' She stood up and opened a door to the left. We entered a short passageway with no windows that led to another door. She opened this and showed me into a small room with a table and two chairs. There was a window, but it was grimy and barred. 'Mr Edward will be with you shortly,' she said and left closing the door behind her. I was relieved not to hear the sound of a key turning.

I went over to the window and tried to make out the view below, but it was too dirty for me to do so. I sat for a while, but found I could not easily stay still, so I contented myself with pacing and thinking about what I would say. By the time Mr Edward entered the room I had convinced myself this was a foolish errand, but had marshalled my facts into good order.

He looked much the same as he had in the Highlands. There was no reason why he should have changed but in this strange and shabby setting I had expected him to be different. But he remained a man in his middle years, with a mild and unprepossessing face except for a pair of extremely bushy eyebrows. He was wearing a very well-cut but underplayed brown suit. His voice, when he spoke, had lost none of its authority.

'Miss Martins, I hear you have been troubled by inconvenient corpses again.'

'Only one corpse so far, Mr Edward. The fate of the other victim hangs in the balance. But I am not at all sure this is something for you. If you are indeed...' I looked around helplessly. '...what you were before.'

Mr Edward chuckled. 'You of all people, Miss Martins, should know that appearances can be deceptive. Have a seat and tell me why this particular puzzle will not interest the bureau.'

I related the facts in order and in some detail as I was unsure what was important and what was not.

'So it is your belief that the message about a lost child was what caused Mrs Wilson distress?'

'I may be making too much of what Dr Simpson said, but I got the impression there was some secret in Mrs Wilson's past. His warning to me also of not allowing history to repeat itself lends credence to the suggestion.'

'Do you know if the late Lord Stapleford's rather eccentric will applied to all his children or only his legitimate heirs?'

117

'I have no idea,' I said startled.

'In my experience most men repeat their mistakes.'

'You mean there may be other children?'

'It is an avenue worth considering.'

'Is it too much to think that Miss Wilton may have pushed the glass?' I asked.

'She is – was – an ambitious young lady. We have been aware of her activities for a while.'

'Do you mean she was a foreign spy?' I asked breathless.

Mr Edward gave a bark of laughter. 'I do enjoy your company, Miss Martins.' He took out a handkerchief and dabbed at one eye. 'No. Merely that in her attempts to become a journalist of note rather than a mere society writer she was asking a lot of awkward questions in a lot of difficult areas. You see, most women of note longed to appear in her column, mentioned favourably, of course, and most women of note...'

'Are married to men of note,' I finished for him.

'I was considering recruiting her,' said Mr Edward. 'She had a fine network of information, but further study suggested her personality as well as her health made her unsuitable for our work.'

I blinked at the word 'our' but decided he was adopting a royal stance.

'The asylum she took you to is one of the very best in the country. Dr Frank is extremely well regarded.'

'I fail to see the connection,' I begun.

'But that is it exactly, Miss Martins. It is all about connections.'

'Miss Wilton kept notes.'

'I shall have them retrieved from the local police force. As to this matter of a second doctor. Was she, in your opinion, the kind of woman who would have told her admirer that the doctor had been merely so he would leave her alone?'

'No, she was the kind of woman who revelled in attention.'

'Perhaps not if she was feeling extremely unwell?' suggested Mr Edward with a fierce frown.

'Sir, my head is going round. I cannot see how all these pieces are connected.'

'Neither can I. But I can see certain lines of enquiry to follow.'

'So you think it is worth pursuing?'

'If there's an outside chance of getting Richard Stapleford under control it's worth investigating.'

'By under control, you mean?'

'I mean what I mean, Miss Martins. The man's a damned loose cannon in more ways than one and now he's a member of parliament he has even more potential for causing harm.'

'What should I do?'

'Return to the hotel and be ready to receive my instructions.'

'Your instructions?'

'Shall we say then my suggestions? You did, after all, come to me for my help.'

'But I thought you would...'

'Deal with it?' said Mr Edward. 'As you said, my dear, the evidence here is extremely thin. I may be able to give you some pointers when I have consulted our files, but I'm afraid that solving this puzzle will be down to you and

119

Bertram Stapleford.'

'But he will be tied up with the funeral arrangements. The family. He couldn't possibly...'

Mr Edward rose. 'Then you will have to find someone else to aid you. Good day, Miss Martins. I will give your grandfather your regards.'

'I'd really rather you didn't,' I said.

Mr Edward smiled slightly and held the door open for me. 'You'll hear from me in due course.'

The young woman at the front desk gave me a cheery goodbye just as if I had come in to be fitted for a coat. I made my way down the dark and dirty staircase wondering what on earth I had got myself involved with.

I arrived back at the hotel to find Bertram in a terrible state. 'Bea's parents are abroad and her brothers are in the country or involved in some business that cannot be left. I'm not sure of the way of it, but in short they have asked that I begin the arrangements for them. Euphemia, I have no idea what to do! I've telephoned to Richard and asked him to send me more staff, but they won't be here for at least a couple of days.'

I pulled my gloves off and threw them down on the table. 'Then you are lucky you have me on your staff, sir, because I have considerable experience in the arrangement of funerals.'

'Euphemia, you are a marvel.'

'Who is Lord Richard sending?' I asked, thinking of the difficulties of keeping Merry and Merrit under control in the circumstances.

'Rory McLeod. Apparently, he was very keen to lend a hand.' Bertram gave me a hard look. 'I can't think why.'

Chapter Eight

Tea with the Butler

The next four days disappeared in a flurry of details and arrangements. Fortunately, this gave Bertram no chance to discover whether I had followed through my plan to visit Mr Edward. When I returned to the hotel I had found him closeted with the local police. I next met him at breakfast when he was consumed with the problems of the arrangements before him and seemed to have forgotten our previous conversation. All his attention was turned to observing the proprieties correctly.

Rory arrived early the second day, but I only heard about this as I was so busy finding the correct venue (in this and other London-related matters, the concierge was able to give me excellent advice.) Then I was sending out the funeral notices. I received constant and demanding telegrams from the Wiltons, who were hotfooting their way across Europe as fast as possible. These communications were naturally addressed to Bertram and just as naturally he passed them back to me to deal with.

For the first time I was able to display to my own satisfaction that I was more than competent to be a private secretary. Being a housekeeper was not a dissimilar task except instead of dealing with a pickling crisis and linen overhauls I was involved in more administrative tasks. There were so many conflicting demands from various relatives that my diplomatic skills, as well as my planning acumen, were tested to the limits. I found it totally absorbing. On several occasions I caught myself up with a guilty start; I was enjoying this and it did not seem appropriate to be enjoying the arrangements of a funeral.

Bertram bent over my paper-laden desk. 'I don't believe Richenda could have done a better job,' he said. 'It was so unfortunate that she has been taken ill and this burden fell on your shoulders, but you have done magnificently. One could almost imagine you were born to this role.'

He meant this kindly and so I did not correct him that his stepsister would not and could not have done half as good a job. Richenda's excuses for not attending had begun with her horse being sick, expanded to Baggy Tipton's continuing presence requiring her to remain as hostess and finally, when all else had failed, she had declared a sick-headache which she felt was liable to develop into either a raging fever or a severe case of the chills. I think even Richard felt she was letting the side down, which was why he had taken the almost unprecedented step of leaving Stapleford Hall without either a housekeeper or a butler when he sent Rory to us.

Before he left Bertram touched me on the shoulder. 'Glad you didn't follow through on the plan of yours last night. We were both shocked and distressed – there's no reason to trouble you-know-who. The local authorities are quite satisfied.'

Of course I should have corrected him at the time, but I can only offer as excuse that my mind was occupied with where to seat the Countess of X, who had unreasonably decided to accept her courtesy invite to the memorial service. If he challenged me later I would say my mind was taken up with the proprieties.

It was shortly before dinner that I was disturbed in the room I had been assigned as a working office. 'Hallo, Euphemia,' said Rory, his voice burring with his soft accent. He was leaning casually in the doorway quite unlike his normal upright posture when he was on duty at Stapleford Hall. 'So this is where you've been hiding. Don't you know there's work to be done, lass?'

An indignant retort sprung to my lips, but I saw the twinkle in his eyes. I rose and went over to shake his hand. 'It's good to see you, Rory.'

Rory took in my desk. 'Have you been arranging everything?' he asked.

'Mr Bertram is almost constantly out with Merrit seeing the arrangements through and visiting people.'

'But you are doing all the formal planning and responding to letters and telegrams?'

I didn't answer.

'Am I right? That man works you like a dog.'

'Oh come, Rory. He's stricken with grief.'

'Guilt more like. He'd only known the woman five minutes, so I cannae believe his heart was engaged. But he certainly should have known not to encourage her in this investigation business.'

'You know about that?'

'Her younger brother lives not far from Stapleford. He came round and made his views known to Lord Stapleford – loudly.'

'Neither he nor his wife were concerned enough to take on the funeral arrangements,' I retorted.

'More than that. Richard is paying for all this. Apparently, Miss Wilton had been denied her heart's desire not because she was a woman, as she fondly believed, but because her family felt her intellect and stamina were not up to a task that would place an intolerable burden upon her.'

'Women being the weaker sex, of course,' I said, my lip curling.

'Euphemia, they were right in this case. The woman died.'

'The hotel doctor said that given her condition she could have died at any time. Bertram said she knew that and she wanted to make the most of her time.'

'Aye, well, I can see that. Just as I can see her family wanted to protect her.'

'Come in, sit down and have some tea,' I said. 'I'll ring for some.'

Rory came in and settled in a comfortable armchair. 'You're quite at home doing this, aren't you?'

'It comes to me more readily than housekeeping, I'll admit, but even that is improving.'

Rory grinned.

'It is.'

'When the house isn't falling down about your ears!'

'Oh that! It all seems a thousand miles away now. The builders should be finished by the time we return.'

Rory's face darkened.

I added quickly. 'How will they manage at the hall without you?'

'I have no idea,' said Rory. 'I've left copious instructions, but it will likely fall on Miss Richenda to issue day-to-day orders to individual staff.'

'It will be chaos!'

'She's not as incapable as she lets people think. She did run the shelter for fallen women in London.'

'I thought she only took an interest.'

Rory shook his head. 'No, she was apparently very heavily involved. Her father's will and her greed for Stapleford Hall changed all that.'

'You don't like her much, do you?'

'She's one of my employers. My liking or disliking is not applicable or appropriate.'

'I've seen Mr Edward,' I said desperately trying to divert Rory from our usual bone of contention. It did not have quite the desired effect.

'You've what!' thundered Rory.

'With the police turning up and us being involved in another strange death I thought I should enlist his advice. He gave me his direction for that very purpose.'

'Strange death?'

'There was some talk of a doctor being here before the doctor actually arrived. Bertram thinks it was Miss Wilton trying to reassure him, but what with our visit to the asylum and the whole séance event and Mrs Wilson's attack I thought there might be something all behind it. He did say...' I trailed off.

'Aye, I suppose you were wise to seek him out.

You have a rare knack of getting into trouble. I take it he told you there was nothing to worry about?'

'Actually he said he'd look into it and get back to me.'

'What?'

'He did say he wouldn't have staff to investigate it himself and that I would have to take any matters into my own hands. As long as I could find someone to help me.'

'Oh no. No way, Euphemia. Last time we got mixed up with that lot we almost got shot and we had to watch a man be executed. That's not something I want to go through again.'

'I'm not sure how much choice I have. I did more or less agree.'

'Euphemia!' exploded Rory.

Fortunately I was saved at this point by the arrival of the tea-tray. It is very difficult for a man of even common breeding who has an ounce of gentility in his soul to be angry around a tea-tray and certainly not a butler: there is the fine china to be considered.

'So what's the story you've concocted in your head this time?' asked Rory.

'I don't have one,' I said bluntly. 'I have only bits and pieces. Mrs Wilson's strange reaction to the séance. Her argument with Lord Richard. Her attack. Miss Wilton's determined pursuit of Bertram. Her interest in the asylum – which I first thought was a hope that she could get Lord Richard incarcerated due to his previous activities, but Bertram assures me he has not divulged any family secrets to her despite her hints to me that he had. Miss Wilton's declaration a doctor had visited when the hotel doctor was across town.'

'Hmm, it doesn't amount to much. Mrs Wilson was – hopefully is – a puritanical old stick and would be shocked at the mention of what I presume was meant to refer to a love-child. Lord Richard was in a foul mood that night. I heard him arguing with Tipton. Tipton even left the hall for a few days until Richenda managed to persuade him back. The attack was probably an opportunist burglar and, as for Miss Wilton's death, it is tragic, but not unexpected. I have no doubt her story about a doctor was merely to assure Mr Bertram. He can be annoyingly persistent.'

I ignored this final comment. 'When did Tipton leave the hall? Was it immediately?'

'No,' said Rory slowly. 'The disagreement dragged on. It was sometime later.'

'Was he at the hall the day Miss Wilton died?'

Rory thought for a moment. 'No.' Then he laughed. 'You're surely not suggesting he came to London and, what? Frightened Miss Wilton to death? I know his fashion sense leaves a lot to be desired, but...'

'Rory, this is not a time to be humorous!'

'Why would he do it?'

'Miss Wilton was closing in on Bertram. He could have thought she'd get Bertram to the altar before he got Richenda there. First one to start a family...'

'It doesn't bear thinking about.'

'No,' I said.

'Good grief,' said Rory.

'What colour are Tipton's eyes?'

'I have no idea,' said Rory. 'Why? You do ask the most extraordinary questions.'

'I saw the eyes of my attacker.'

'Then you must tell the police!'

'I did,' I responded. 'Sergeant Davies advised me to keep the information to myself until the investigation had progressed further.'

'He thought you were in danger?' asked Rory aghast.

'I think so. Which is why I was keen to come to London with Mr Bertram. But I fear the danger has followed us.'

'Did Miss Wilton keep a notebook?' asked Rory with that quickness of mind I found so stimulating.

'Yes. I told Mr Edward this, but I fear the local police have taken it.'

'And Mr Bertram had no idea what she was investigating?'

I shook my head.

'So where do we go from here?' asked Rory.

'Wherever Mr Edward sends us,' I replied.

'Wherever that may be,' muttered Rory darkly, but I was heartened to hear he did not correct my pronoun. It was a tacit agreement to help. But then I knew he would never let me go into danger alone. Really, I was as manipulative as Miss Wilton.

I got my answer sooner than I expected. A telegram arrived the next morning from AE. It said:

Advise visiting _____ Asylum in the county

128

of_____. Late SS advisor and regular donator. Noted in family papers.

AE

There was no mention of Miss Wilton's notebook. I sighed. How exactly was I meant to travel so far? I would have no choice but to show the telegram to Mr Bertram and I rather feared that in his current mood he would forbid me to go, which would make the journey all the more awkward. I decided to seek Rory's advice.

'There's only one way we can do this, Euphemia,' he said casting his eyes over the paper. 'We'll have to take the automobile.'

'But Bertram?'

'You've not told him?'

I shook my head. 'I told him of my intention to visit Mr Edward, but he appears to think it was only my natural shock and distress at discovering yet another corpse.'

'Doesn't know you as well as he thinks he does, does he?' said Rory a trifle smugly.

'His mind is elsewhere, but not sufficiently that we can confiscate his vehicle. Why he is out in it most days!'

'He'll be part of the funeral cortege, won't he?'

'We can't! Not then!'

'They'll never notice if you're at the back of the church or not,' said Rory. 'You certainly won't be getting any thanks for all the work you've done.'

'But I need to pay my respects.'

'You didn't like the woman.'

'All the more reason,' I said stubbornly. 'I regret I wasn't kinder.'

'Look at it this way; you're honouring her by following her line of enquiry.'

'But I don't know that this *was* her line of enquiry!'

'If Mr Edward is advising you to go there then you can be assured it's something to do with this mess. It can't be coincidence that it's another asylum he's suggesting.'

'Merrit will have to drive. What do we tell him?'

'Leave that to me,' said Rory.

I did not at all like our plan and on several occasions I determined to tell Mr Bertram all, but each time we spoke, and this was far from frequently, he was clearly preoccupied and grieving. I, in turn, was unreasonably short tempered because of my guilt and, in short, our relationship – whatever it was – was not going well. The day of the funeral advanced relentlessly towards us and I knew I could not tell him on such short notice. Rory had been most noticeable in his absence from my office.

It was the afternoon before Miss Beatrice Wilton's memorial service and of our clandestine adventure when Rory reappeared with a tea-tray.

'I've something to tell yous and I think yer gonna need a biscuit,' he said depositing the tray on my table in the middle of my papers.

'Rory!'

'Donna tell me meist of the work is not already done?'

'You're being alarmingly Scotch,' I said. 'What's the matter?'

'I had a wee thought about yon Tipton being away from the hall. I don't know if you know this but there are several men's servants' clubs in the city. I managed to track down the one Tipton's valet belongs to and, after a sufficient number of pints, I managed to extract some information from the man. Seems Tipton had sent him back to town when he learned of the funeral.'

'Rory, you're a marvel.'

'Aye, well,' said Rory pouring the tea. 'It wasnae that hard. The man fair loathes his master and was well up to moan about him. I tried not to make my questions too direct, so I got a lot of useless stuff about Tipton's vanity and his weak nature.'

'It might not be useless,' I said. 'Anything that gives us insight into his behaviour.'

'There was a lot of talk about how Tipton would come to his room and shout about how unfair the world was to him. How no one appreciated what he did for them. Not many specifics. A lot of rage against Lord Stapleford.'

'That he wouldn't ever say to his face! What a coward.'

'Don't forget he was arguing with him on the night of Mrs Wilson's attack. Although, from what the valet said that does seem very out of character.'

'Like he'd reached breaking point?'

Rory nodded. 'What's more he'd been known to throw things at the valet when in a temper. Typical action of a coward. Striking someone who cannot strike back.'

'Was the man hurt?' I asked in horror.

'No, he said all Tipton's servants knew they needed to be nippy on their feet when he was in a mood. But it was more brushes or glasses. Small things that lay to hand. I understand they keep his apartments especially tidy.'

'I see,' I said thoughtfully. 'So a man who might lash out in rage, but not a fighter.'

'But there's more,' said Rory. 'It turns out Tipton was in town on the day Miss Wilton died. The valet says Tipton was in a right mood about coming up as if it wasn't his idea at all, but it was all done in a terrible rush. It quite caught him out because he'd been in London only two months ago between the 12th and 19th and Tipton had sworn he hated the place and was never coming back. And guess where he stayed?'

'Here,' I said.

'Correct,' said Rory.

'Are we really suggesting Tipton could be a killer?' I asked.

'Weak men can surprise you when they are pushed hard enough, but I can't see it myself.'

'You don't happen to remember what colour his eyes are, do you?'

'Ach, Euphemia, it's rare to notice anyone's eye colour. It's one of those things you see all the time, but tend not to pay attention to.' He turned his head away. 'What's mine?'

'Why, green,' I said astonished. As if anyone could miss his strangely luminous and attractive eyes. 'What's mine?'

'Grey,' he said gruffly.

I felt myself blushing. 'I suppose we have been in each other's company much more frequently than either of us has been with Mr Tipton.'

'I suppose so,' said Rory.

'I cannot believe Tipton is a killer. Besides, what reason would he have?'

'Tipton,' said Rory slowly, 'is very much Lord Stapleford's pawn.'

'Richenda.'

'Aye, maybe. She'll be a rich woman soon.'

'Isn't she already?'

Rory pulled a face. 'I don't like spreading gossip.'

'What have you heard? It might be important.'

'You know the late Lord Stapleford set up a mighty odd bit in his will?'

I nodded impatiently. 'We've been over this.'

'Aye, but that's about the hall and grounds. There's a lot more to the Staplefords than that.'

'Of course,' I said feeling very stupid. 'The bank and armaments investments.'

'I don't rightly know what it is, but I do know both brothers received their share on the death of their father.'

A cold chill swept down my back – so that was how Bertram had bought White Orchards! After all his protestations about not using or accepting blood money!

'However,' Rory continued, 'Miss Richenda, being a woman, has to wait until she reaches a suitable age. This autumn, it turns out. Until then her money is held in trust by her brother. But if she marries, it will go directly to her husband's control.'

'What!' I gasped astonished.

'It's the normal way of things, Euphemia.'

'But that's terrible! How did you find out?'

'Merry heard her raging about it.'

'And told you?'

'You know Merry and I were getting along. I told you I fancied she wanted a wee bit more. Which is why I was gey glad Merrit appeared on the scene. She's a lovely lass, but not my type at all. Besides, it wouldn't have been professional.'

'Of course not,' I said coldly. 'We servants are not allowed lives of our own, let alone relationships.'

'Would you want one?' asked Rory.

'I hope one day to marry and have my own family,' I said as evenly as I could.

'I'll bear that in mind,' said Rory.

I felt myself blushing from my head to my toes.

Chapter Nine

A Stapleford Secret

'I'm sorry, sir,' I said gently. 'I don't believe it would be proper.'

'Fine. Suit yourself.' Bertram turned on his heel and walked away quickly without a backward glance.

Rory appeared beside me. 'Did I hear the man asking you to be his escort for the funeral?'

I nodded. There was a lump in my throat too large to speak.

'The man's out of his mind! You're a servant not his equal.'

'I don't think he sees it like that.'

'Well, he should,' said Rory angrily.

'I like that about him,' I said equally angrily.

'Good God, Euphemia! Don't you see? Everyone would think you were his mistress! And besides the sheer bad manners of bringing his mistress to his lover's funeral it would ruin your reputation for life!'

'His mistress?' I gasped.

'I'm the one who used to belong to the communist party and I wouldn't do such a thing in his position. You're constantly courting disaster around that man. He doesn't think.'

I bowed my head. 'I believe you were right when you told me not to accept the position at White Orchards.'

'Aye, well,' said Rory in a mollified tone. 'Now the nobs are away let's get on with the real business of today.'

Merrit was waiting for us in the automobile. Rory opened the door and handed me in. He tapped on the glass and Merrit drove off without a word.

'I told him where we're going,' said Rory, 'but not why. He won't ask any questions.'

All men like to have some mystery about them, so I didn't enquire further. I preferred not to think about the possibility that Rory might be proposing poaching one of my staff. I suspected from the way Merrit's face lit up whenever Merry was mentioned that he might do a great deal to be with her. Better, of course, would be for Merry to transfer to White Orchards. But could I really have my old friend and colleague as a junior member of my staff? I mused over this for

135

some time when Rory, who had been equally lost in thought, suddenly said, 'Have you considered what we will do when we get there?'

'No,' I said. The realisation made me feel very foolish. 'I was hoping that things would resolve themselves.'

'That isn't like you,' said Rory, not unkindly.

'When *things* have happened before it's all been quick and dangerous and often dark without candlesticks.'

Rory grinned. 'That's one way of describing our adventure in the Highlands.'

'There's been more than that,' I said quietly. 'When that attacker knocked me to the ground it was quite like old times. When poor Miss Wilton died it was different. We still don't know if there was anything nefarious about her demise, but I have this nagging feeling that something is very wrong.'

'And how accurate are your feelings generally?' asked Rory still smiling.

'My instincts are frequently acute, but my surmises based on these sometimes in error.'

'That's very honest.'

I sighed. 'I know you don't want to hear this, Rory, but I cannot help but feel that behind all this is the hand of Richard Stapleford. He has become like some dark monster to me and I fancy I see his shadow everywhere.'

'Isn't that a little melodramatic? I admit he's not a likable man, but he seems no worse to me than many masters.'

'He works in armaments and banking and was raised in blood money. He has few scruples and has recently become a member of parliament.'

'How apt,' murmured Rory.

'But Mr Bertram and I suspect he murdered his own father.' There, it was said. It was out there. I waited for Rory to protest. He didn't.

'We had good reason to believe it. Enough evidence to convince a police inspector to arrest him.'

'So why isn't he in jail?'

'When I say evidence I mean we had pieces of the puzzle. We could make a convincing argument he had done it. And the fact that Richenda and he had kidnapped me and locked me in a cupboard added to the conviction, but in the end when the case was reviewed it was decided there wasn't enough evidence to prosecute.'

'They locked you in a cupboard?'

'Yes.'

'They presumably know you believe this of them?'

'I don't believe Richenda knows or cares what happened to her father, but she is loyal to her twin.'

'For God's sake if even half of this is true why haven't you left the Staplefords?'

'I went to White Orchards.'

'So you don't believe your Bertram is involved in the death of his father in any way?'

'We were working together to try and prove his brother's guilt.'

'You can't tell me that wouldn't have been convenient for him?'

'I think you're right this is all about inheritance,' I said evenly. 'That and the money Richard hopes

137

to make should there be a war.'

'Should there be a war?' Rory looked aghast.

'I believe much of Mr Edward's interest concerns a fear that Richard will be investing in and selling weaponry to the wrong side. The Germans. In this I think he is mistaken. I do suspect that Richard favours the German empire over our own for philosophical reasons, but I think he is more than happy to supply weaponry to both.'

'I'm a butler,' said Rory. 'This is beyond me and it should be beyond you. Why on earth haven't you got as far away from the Staplefords as you could?'

'It has been suggested,' I said carefully, 'that any trip I took might end precipitously and not well.'

'You mean Richard would arrange to have you killed?'

'If any of the surmises we have spoken of are correct it seems a possibility I would be foolish to discount.'

'Then why...' Rory paused. 'This is incredible. Are you suggesting the man keeps you around to keep an eye on you?'

'It would be too inconvenient to kill me on his own doorstep. The number of deaths surrounding the Staplefords have already drawn a lot of attention. Their friends can only keep so much quiet.'

Rory rubbed his hand through his hair much to the disturbance of his elegant blond locks. 'This is all a bit thick,' he said sounding rather dazed.

'I should have told you all this before, but I

didn't want,' I wanted to say 'to drive you away', but instead I said, 'to put you in danger.'

'Which this trip is likely to do?'

'If Lord Richard hears about it,' I said, 'I suppose it might.'

'If there is something to discover here then it will undoubtedly put us all in danger.' He nodded significantly at Merrit in the chauffeur's seat. 'How much does Merry know?'

'Nothing.'

'Very wise.'

Rory lapsed into silence. An apology seemed a poor offering for the danger I had placed him in, so I kept silent too. Many miles later he said, 'What do we hope to find at this place?'

I showed him the telegram. 'You still think the late Lord Stapleford and Mrs Wilson had a love child, don't you?'

'Dr Simpson implied they did.'

'But what does it matter?' asked Rory.

'Social embarrassment for a member of parliament?' I suggested.

'The scandal of his father's love life might be more detrimental to his business interests than the fact he is a suspected murderer?'

'I have never understood politics, but I think it might be so.'

Rory rubbed his head again. 'You could be right. Although I think there is one possibility you overlook.'

'What is that?'

'What if Lord Stapleford married Mrs Wilson?'

'If he had he would have had no reason to ship her child off to an asylum.'

139

'And what woman would stay with a man who did that?' asked Rory.

'Perhaps the child really is mad.'

'And you're sure Mrs Wilson never spoke of this to anyone? I would have thought Mrs Deighton as the longest-serving member of staff might know something.'

'She never said a word to me, but then I was hardly there any time at all in terms of the family's occupancy.'

'You're right, we're going to have to play this entirely on the hoof,' said Rory. 'I suggest we pretend to be brother and sister making enquires of a private, family nature.'

'You mean that we have someone in the family we want to lock up?'

'Exactly,' said Rory.

'Perhaps our father knew the late Lord Stapleford?'

'And advised us to come here,' completed Rory.

We both took a deep breath as the automobile rolled through the gates of the asylum.

The drive was not that different to that of any leading to a substantial country house. The building itself emerged through the trees not modern, but of cheerful aspect. Merrit opened Rory's door and he then handed me down. I was still taking in the many gables, the extensive lawns – indeed the scale of the place – when the sound of childish laughter reached my ears. I turned to Rory astonished. 'Didn't you see,' he whispered in my ear, 'the sign as we entered the drive? This is an asylum for children.'

'How could anyone be so cruel?' I exclaimed hotly.

Rory pressed my hand hard. The door at the top of a grand stone staircase had opened and a middle-aged woman, in a neat black dress, was making her way towards us.

She smiled in greeting and held out her hand. 'Would you be Lord Stapleford's relatives?' she enquired.

'Yes,' said Rory before I could prevent him. 'We are.'

'It's so nice to meet you. I am Mrs Mason. I'm the matron here. If you wish I could get one of the medical staff to show you around, but I thought for your purposes a more informal approach might be better. And of course I do know all my charges very well.'

'Children in an asylum,' I exclaimed, no longer able to contain myself. 'It is tragic.'

Mrs Mason bridled slightly. 'We do our very best to give them a happy childhood. I often think they're better off than all those wee ones that live on the streets. It's not as if they could manage in the big, wide world themselves. No family however loving can be expected to cope with these kind of difficulties. I like to think we do the Lord's work.'

I gaped, astonished at this speech.

'Is that a wee Scottish burr I hear in your voice, Mrs Mason?' asked Rory. 'I'm from the Highlands myself.'

The tension in the air evaporated. 'You don't say, sir? I didn't know the Staplefords had a Scottish connection.'

141

'I'm a distant relative,' said Rory suavely. 'Here to escort my young cousin. It's really for her that we're here.'

'Oh, I am sorry, my dear,' said Mrs Mason. 'But it can happen to any mother.'

I cast my eyes down and tried to look suitably tragic. I made a mental note not to remove my gloves and display my ringless hand. Really, this was a ridiculous game. Every sentence she uttered took us deeper into the mire. I was relieved that Rory had not seen fit to mention our names, but should the Staplefords enquire over this visit I feared our descriptions would be all too easy to recognise. The only thing to do was to get through the visit as smoothly as possible, so Mrs Mason had no reason to contact the real family.

'So I am often told,' I said reverting to my real accent and sounding like the earl's granddaughter I am.

Mrs Mason came up and took one of my hands in hers. 'Your husband not with you, my dear?'

'He leaves such matters to me.'

'Men!' exclaimed Mrs Mason in an exasperated, breathy voice. 'Still you have your fine Scottish cousin with you.'

I nodded and tried to bring a tear to my eye.

Mrs Mason patted my hand. 'It's a wee bit chilly, but I think you'd enjoy seeing the children at play. Could you be persuaded to walk a while, my dear?'

'Certainly, if you think it best,' I said in a subdued voice.

'This way then and you can meet some of my charges.'

142

Instead of taking us through the house Mrs Mason led us round the substantial left wing and down along a wooded path. As we progressed the sound of laughter became louder. Finally, we turned a corner and came across four children aged between, I imagine, four and eight, playing with a hoop and stick and watched over by a young woman, also in a black dress. At first glance there was nothing different from what one might have seen in any park up and down the country.

'Go forward, my dear,' said Mrs Mason. 'They're a friendly lot.'

Out of the corner of my eye I saw her place a restraining hand on Rory's arm. I stopped a little distance from the children as if I was studying them, but ensuring I could still overhear her conversation with Rory. A little girl with a sweet but vacant face suddenly sat down at my feet engrossed in playing with a loose ribbon. The others did not seem to notice she was missing. I knelt down beside her.

'That's a pretty ribbon,' I said.

The child laughed and pointed at my face. 'Ah-gog,' she said. Then continued in a stream of happy babble. She must have been six years old and was clearly without speech. Carefully I retied the bow for her and she looked at me with such openness and trust that a genuine tear came to my eye.

'Leave her be,' Mrs Mason was saying to Rory. 'It's important for the mothers to see we treat them as normally as we can. She's very young. I take it the poor wee one is a tiny mite?'

143

'Aye,' said Rory promptly. 'A few months.'

'And you could tell already,' said Mrs Mason. 'The poor lady. But she's young. She'll have others.'

'I believe the child has the same condition as...'

'Lord Stapleford's niece?' finished Mrs Mason.

'It's never been discussed, you understand, but one hears things.'

'A six months' child, so sad. A very sweet nature and the face of an angel. She grew into a truly beautiful woman. When she came to us she wasn't expected to live. Such a tiny thing. But she did. Tenacious, that's what Dr Frank called it, a tenacious desire to live. But the kindest, most gentle being alive. If you took it slow she could understand most things. Such a shame her mother never felt up to visiting her, but then so many don't. I still miss her.'

'When did she...?'

'Oh, at 18, like all of them.'

'I see,' said Rory in a bemused voice. 'At 18.'

'At least she had Alice to go with her. She was a particular friend.'

'I see,' said Rory, swallowing.

'Oh, they're quite capable of friendship and affection. That's why they're such a particular charge when they're grown.'

'You mean she transferred elsewhere?' The relief in Rory's voice was evident.

'Oh yes! This place is only for children. When they're grown they go to an adult institution, but we do our best to ensure they are placed in the most modern places run on similar ideas to ourselves. Care, compassion, exercise and pleasant usefulness. Sometimes they can be trained to live simply in the outside world, but in Sophy's case that simply wasn't possible. She'd been in an institution all her life and besides, if a mother doesn't want a child home, there really is nothing one can do. Do you think?'

'I don't think she has yet made her decision,' said Rory.

The little girl ran away from me and back to the group with the hoop. The young woman in black smiled encouragingly at me, but I shook my head. I was already feeling uncomfortable about our subterfuge and the innocent, happy cries of the children were making me feel worse. One little boy turned his face towards me and I saw the difference marked clearly upon it. He had beautiful, clear eyes and a lopsided smile. I retreated back towards Rory.

'Come inside,' said Mrs Mason. 'I'll show you around. Most of our inmates are at play or work, so we won't be intruding. We do our best not to make them feel they are being inspected.'

I smiled. This was a far cry from the horror tales of Old Bedlam. The inside of the building was much as we might have expected. There were long dormitories for the separate sexes for the younger children and a selection of single rooms for older residents, whose relatives could afford a larger donation, and who it was felt would benefit from isolation. 'Most of them prefer to be in the dormitories,' Mrs Mason assured us. There were large open schoolroom workshop type places where the children were taught occupations according to their abilities. It was a place full of

145

bright light, open spaces and cheerfulness. Mrs Mason told us it was inspired by the Quaker values and the central focus was to make the children feel as if they were part of one big, happy and productive family.

'This is a more idyllic childhood than many children achieve,' I said sincerely.

'You must bear in mind that the understanding of many of our charges is severely limited. What seems to you tranquil may still feel overbearing to some of them.'

I nodded sadly. 'But after this?'

Mrs Mason hung her head. 'Many of them do feel it is a wrench to leave and I feel for them. But the difficulties of looking after simple adults and the temptations that attend them mean that they need a special kind of care.'

'We very much appreciate your time, Mrs Mason,' said Rory as we enjoyed a final cup of tea in her office. 'I think it would ease my cousin's mind if we would also see the institution that Sophy moved on to.'

'Of course,' said Mrs Mason. 'I'll write the address down for you.' She penned a few lines and passed them over to Rory. 'And please let me say I was so sorry to hear about Sophy. She was a lovely girl, but then the Lord often sees fit to gather these special ones to himself early.'

My cup rattled in my saucer.

'Oh, I've spoken out of turn,' said Mrs Mason. 'There really is no reason to think your child won't enjoy a long and happy life, my dear.'

'Unlike poor Sophy,' I said quietly.

Chapter Ten

Mrs Wilson's Bargain

'I must tell Bertram,' I said.

We were back in the automobile.

'Then we will have to tell him everything we have done. He won't be happy,' said Rory.

'He needs to know he had a half-sister.'

Rory took my hand. 'We don't know for certain Sophy was his sister.' I opened my mouth to protest, but he forestalled me. 'I agree we have every reason to be suspicious, but we don't have any proof, do we?'

I looked down at his hand in mine. I knew my mother would be appalled at this familiarity, but all I saw in Rory's face was a deep concern. 'We could be in danger, couldn't we?' I said.

'Of losing our situations certainly,' answered Rory. 'As for anything else. Yes, I agree we might know potentially damaging information about the Staplefords or we may only have uncovered that the late Lord Stapleford made proper arrangements for his unfortunate niece.'

'But she's dead, Rory.'

'Mrs Mason was quite clear that those that God has made differently often do not live long lives.'

'I know, but I cannot but fear...'

'That Richard Stapleford killed her? But what

reason would he have?'

'Scandal?'

'Do we know the exact wording of the late Lord Stapleford's will?'

'Bert-Mr Bertram said the first legitimate heir of his children would inherit the estate and a trust to run it.'

'It would only matter if there was any chance of her being released from the asylum, marrying and having a child. It's a bit of a stretch,' said Rory.

'From what Mrs Mason says that seems un-likely,' I said. 'Besides she is illegitimate, so wouldn't that rule her out?'

'It would depend on how the will was worded.'

'Unless he married Mrs Wilson,' I said.

'I think we can discount that possibility, don't you?'

'It does seem the most farfetched of all the ideas we have discussed,' I agreed.

'Aye, it's a strange world where murder to prevent scandal is more likely than marrying for love,' said Rory.

'I cannot imagine Mrs Wilson ever being lov-able!'

'I'm sure she was young once,' said Rory.

'I fear she was merely convenient.'

'You don't think much of the Staplefords, do you?'

'I have no reason to think well of any of the noble families of my acquaintance,' I said truth-fully.

'And you know so many?' teased Rory.

I took a deep breath. 'Rory,' I said, 'there's

something you don't know about me.'

'Aye, lass. I've always suspected you had a secret or two. But is now the right time to tell me? We've got enough on our plates as it is, don't you think?'

'Oh, I don't know. My head is spinning with all this. I want to be honest with someone.'

'Will it change things between us?'

'It might,' I admitted.

'Yer no married to Mr Bertram, are ye?'

I laughed out loud. 'Oh no, it's nothing as awful as that!'

Rory's eyes twinkled. 'In that case if it's something that's going to open up another long discussion I think we should leave it for now. Tell me after all this. If you still want to.'

'All right.'

'I'll remember you wanted to tell me,' said Rory.

'That's good.'

'So where do you think we go from here?'

'You're right. We need some proof of something.'

'We could go back to the asylum.'

'Back?'

Rory showed me the address. 'Didn't you realise the asylum Sophy was sent to was the one Beatrice wanted to investigate? Mrs Mason mentioned Dr Frank.'

'Beatrice was further along in the investigation than we are.'

'Aye, it was a right shame about her.'

'I hope so,' I said under my breath.

We arrived back in London towards evening. Merrit dropped us off at the hotel and took the automobile round to the garage without a word. I found his singular lack of curiosity unnerving, but Rory took it in his stride. 'He's a model servant,' was his comment. 'Doesn't ask any questions.'

The memorial service was long over, so I steeled myself to face a barrage of questions from Mr Bertram. However, when I enquired of him from the concierge I learned he had not yet returned to the hotel. I left a message at the front desk that I was to be called when he returned and retired to my room. I meant to only close my eyes for a moment, but travelling is remarkably fatiguing. I was dreaming that Beatrice Wilton and I were in a crowded dining room. She was trying to tell me something important as she passed me a cup of tea, but the sound of other diners clattering cutlery and chatting drowned out her words. She was becoming increasingly agitated. I, on the other hand, was consumed with the necessity of explaining one never drank tea with dinner. Finally with an expression of exasperation Beatrice slammed a book down upon the table making the dishes jump and startling the room into silence.

I woke up on the edge of the sound unsure if what I had heard was real or still in the dream. My curtains, undrawn, showed a night-black sky. The room was full of shadows and I had the eeriest feeling I was not alone. My heart knocked loudly in my chest and my breath caught in my throat. By sheer effort of will I lay perfectly still. I reasoned if the intruder had not harmed me, believing I was asleep, then they might well depart leaving me unmolested. I squinted into the darkness. Without light my room seemed preternaturally enlarged. I could see nothing but the shapes of the furniture.

A sharp knocking at the door brought me bolt upright. 'Help,' I squeaked.

The door, which I had foolishly left unlocked, opened. Rory stood on the threshold and the gas light from the hall flooded in.

'There's someone in here,' I cried, springing from the bed and running towards him.

Rory turned up the gas. There was no one there.

'I think you've had a bad dream, lass,' said Rory.

'I was so sure,' I said sheepishly.

'Dreams can be powerful things,' he said kindly, leading me into the room. We sat either side of the cold fire. 'I'm sorry to disturb you, but I've had a thought that might help us.'

'Is Mr Bertram back?' I asked.

'I've had no word, but I imagine he must be.'

'I left word I was to be sent for when he returned.'

'It's late, Euphemia. He may have superseded your instructions.'

'I suppose so, but it's odd.'

'It's hardly a normal time.'

'But what will he have been doing?'

Rory sighed. 'I don't know. I imagine he's been with Miss Wilton's family. There will have been many questions. For all I know the family is demanding an inquest.'

'But wouldn't they have had to do that before she was buried?'

'It was a memorial service today, wasn't it?'

'Yes,' I rubbed my eyes. 'Of course. There is still time. What did you want to see me about?'

151

'We need some evidence one way or another and I've thought of someone who can give us some?'

'Who?'

'Mrs Wilson.'

'But she's in a coma.'

'Not any more. Word came to the hall before I left that she was improving. I heard Dr Simpson tell Lord Richard she was having periods of lucidity.'

'But then she could be in the most terrible danger!'

Rory produced a pamphlet from his pocket. 'I don't think we can get away with borrowing the automobile again, but we could get a train to the town where the hospital is. There's a milk train that leaves in two hours that would get us there this morning. If we caught the afternoon train back we'd only be gone the day. Your Mr Bertram might not even notice we were missing. We could leave word we had business out of town.'

'He won't like it,' I said.

'I think we've gone too far to turn back now,' said Rory. 'If we're right we'll come back with proof he had a half-sister. He will have to be interested in that.'

'And if we're wrong?'

'We'll need to look for different situations,' said Rory grimly. 'But I don't think we are wrong.'

'No, neither do I,' I said quietly. 'I wish we were. If we're right then the chances are neither her death, nor Miss Wilton's, was natural.'

'The train leaves in two hours. I've arranged for a carriage to call in an hour. Can you be ready?'

'Of course,' I said. 'Thank you, Rory. I can't imagine doing this without you.'

It is alarming how quickly one adapts to the modern era. I found the horse carriage that took us to the station extremely uncomfortable. As Rory paid off the driver my teeth chattered in my head as much from the bumpy journey as from the cold. The drive through London had been full of mist and shadows. On another occasion I might have found it romantic in the picturesque sense, but this morning the world was full of menace. I constantly fancied we were being followed. Even Rory's patience was on the verge of breaking and he had given up reassuring me. My dream of the night before dragged at my mind.

'Why is milk going from London to the country?' I asked suddenly.

'It's not,' said Rory. 'This is the train going out to pick up the milk for London.'

'What time is it?'

'You don't want to know. There's one passenger carriage. I don't expect it will be that comfortable, but you should try and sleep.'

'I don't think that will be a problem,' I said yawning. 'Maybe I'll be able to recapture that dream.'

Rory muttered something under his breath that I decided not to hear. We made our way onto the platform. This was not the first time I had travelled by train, but as we approached the great, steaming beast I felt my heart flutter. That such a huge engine could reach such great speeds with only the aid of fire and water reminded me of the power of the natural world. There was much about this new century that I loved, but man's desire to master the elements unnerved me. The train snorted steam as we approached our carriage. I could not suppress a fantasy that it was somehow aware. Rory handed me up the steps past the enormous iron wheels that would propel us forward across what during my father's youth would have been unimaginable distances to cross in a day and we would traverse in a few short hours. I snuggled down into my seat, under a blanket Rory had provided, closed my eyes and, with what I felt was more than a little cowardice, banished my surroundings from my thoughts. There was an enormous hiss, the carriage jolted and we were on our way.

Beatrice Wilton was still shouting at me in my dreams when we reached our journey's end. Rory had to shake me awake I was so tired.

'You should see a doctor,' he said. 'I think you're still having effects from your concussion.'

'I'd be fine if Beatrice would shut up,' I snapped.

'I think I should find us transport,' said Rory looking up and down the emptying platform. 'It's only a couple of miles, so I was going to suggest we walked, but you don't look at all well.'

The train station was small with only two platforms, but it was respectable with a high glass-panelled ceiling. There was a first-class ladies' waiting room and the green benches were freshly painted. 'How large is the town? Could we not find a trolleybus or something?'

'Let's look,' said Rory.

We walked out of the station. I cannot easily explain the sense of freedom I felt standing there. I had no luggage. I was miles from my family. I was distant from my employer. All I had was Rory's companionship and a sense of being on an adventure. I would not have minded if I had had to walk five miles.

Fortunately, I did not have to test this resolve. The train station opened out into a busy town centre complete with trolleybus stands. It was most efficiently set up to convey the steam train passengers quickly into the heart of the town. 'I did not realise Stapleford was so near to this metropolis,' I said as we boarded our trolleybus.

'Did you think the Staplefords would build themselves a new property in the middle of nowhere? The house is less than 50 years old.'

'I suppose not. It's just that when you're there, there seems to be nothing around but fields.'

'That's the idea,' said Rory.

The trolleybus moved off with comforting smoothness and took us towards the hospital district. In a short while we were walking up the drive of the hospital. It was a large grey building with small windows and gabled ends. Inside the corridors gleamed and the wooden doors that led from ward to ward shone with polish. The place smelled of carbolic soap and other more pungent chemicals. We had hardly entered the building before a woman in a starched uniform bore down on us.

'Visiting hours are not for another 75 minutes,' she said in a commanding voice.

'I'm sorry,' said Rory. 'We've travelled from

155

London to see a patient. It's an urgent matter.'

'I don't care where you are from, hospital rules apply.'

'Excuse me, matron,' I said, 'but I believe the patient we are visiting may be under different rules. Her name is Mrs Wilson.'

'Are you with the police?'

'Not exactly,' I said, 'but we are helping with enquiries.'

'Hmm,' said the matron. 'It will be up to the police sergeant. Follow me, please.'

She set off at a smart pace, her shoes clacking loudly on the polished floor. Rory and I followed her down a series of corridors until we reached a door with a very bored-looking police officer sitting on a chair outside.

'Visitors for Mrs Wilson,' said the matron tersely. Then she turned on her heel and left us with the startled sergeant.

'I'm Euphemia St John and this is Rory McLeod, we work at Stapleford Hall. We've come down from London to see Mrs Wilson. It's very important.'

The sergeant began to shake his head. 'She's not said a word. Not even to identify her attacker.'

'Has she lost the power of speech?' I asked.

'Doctors don't reckon so,' said the sergeant. 'But she's silent as the grave.'

'Ask her if she wants to see us,' urged Rory. 'Tell her we know about Sophy.'

'This could make all the difference,' I said.

'And if she does want to see us,' said Rory, 'you could away and get yourself a cup of coffee. You

156

look like you've been here all night.'

'And when you come back we could have broken your case. The inspector would be pleased, wouldn't he?'

The sergeant looked from one of us to the other. 'I must be mad. Wait here.' The policeman disappeared into the room.

'That was clever,' I said.

Rory smiled wryly. The sergeant returned quickly. 'She'll see you. She went right pale when I mentioned this Sophy. You'll have to make a full report after you've seen her. And not too long or that ruddy matron will have my guts for garters.'

Mrs Wilson's room was one of those strange hospital chambers that are smallish and square, but with very high ceilings. The walls were painted a colour lost somewhere between a dull grey and green. The simple ironwork bed seemed very small in the centre of the room. Mrs Wilson lay among the sheets, her face almost as pale as the bleached cotton. She had always been thin, but her arms now clearly showed the outline of the bones that lay beneath. Purple bruises flowered on her forearms and a thick yellow bandage was wrapped around her head. Her dark eyes sparked with hostility. Her lips were faint lines and when she spoke her voice was low and rough.

'What do you want?'

There was one chair in the room, a simple wooden affair. Rory pulled it up to the bed for me and stood behind. 'We need to talk to you about what's happening,' I said.

'Why? What's it to you?'

I thought of appealing to her sense of justice, of

157

telling her of Beatrice's death, of our suspicions of patricide and corruption, but I sensed that all would mean little to her. 'You had a child, didn't you?'

Mrs Wilson turned her face away from me.

'She was born at six months,' I continued. 'She was the illegitimate daughter of the late Lord Stapleford.'

Still she said nothing, but I saw her shoulders shake. There was nothing for it but to open up the wound at once.

'You were told she died at birth,' I said levelly, 'but she didn't.'

Mrs Wilson turned to face me. Her face was a mask of rage. 'You lie!'

I shook my head. 'I wish I did. I think he meant to be kind. The doctor, Dr Simpson, didn't think she would live, but she did. She was never – quite right.'

'Deformed?' said Mrs Wilson with horror.

'No. Simple. Trusting. Affectionate.'

'The people who looked after her as a child spoke of her very highly,' broke in Rory.

'Where was this?' The rage in her voice was gone and instead her voice was that of a confused old woman.

'In a children's institution in the country. It's a lovely place.'

'You've been there?'

I nodded.

'Is she there now?' Hope was written clearly across her face.

I shook my head.

'Of course, she'd be grown now,' whispered Mrs

Wilson to herself. 'Where did they send her?'

'I'm so sorry,' I said quietly.

'So she is dead.'

'Yes.'

'Are you enjoying tormenting me?' Her eyes moved to Rory. 'I could believe that of her, but you? There's nothing between us.'

'We need your help,' said Rory.

'We don't believe she died any more naturally than her father,' I said.

'You mean she was murdered?' gasped Mrs Wilson. 'When?'

'We don't know, but we think quite recently,' said Rory.

'She was alive. All this time.' Mrs Wilson's eyes focused into the distance. 'Is that what he meant? That he didn't know about her?'

'Who didn't know?' Rory asked.

Mrs Wilson reached forward and clutched my hand in a vice-like grip. 'Do you think it was her at the séance?'

'I think it was Beatrice Wilton pushing the glass,' I said.

'No. No. It must have been her. You believe, don't you?' She appealed to Rory.

'I don't know, but perhaps,' said Rory. 'My grandmother had the sight and stranger things.'

'We think Richard Stapleford is involved,' I cut in. 'We think he killed or had his half-sister killed for the same reason he murdered his father. For his inheritance.'

'But she had no claim on the family,' said Mrs Wilson. 'When I was pregnant Lord Stapleford told me she would be provided for – and you say that he did that. That he saw she was looked after?'

'Yes,' I said gently. 'She had the best care.'

'Was it expensive? Was that it? Could he no longer pay the bills? I can't believe that. He was always a mean boy, but...' Her voice trailed off.

'He may have been afraid of the scandal now he is in parliament,' I said.

'What did you mean he didn't know?' asked Rory. 'Did you mean that before the séance he didn't know about her at all? That his father never told him?'

Mrs Wilson screwed up her eyes and took several deep breaths. Then she opened them and raised her head with obvious effort. Her voice when she spoke was firm and clear. 'You don't know what happened, do you? You're sticking your oars in stirring up muck and seeing what floats to the surface. If you had anything on Richard Stapleford you'd have taken it to the police by now. Or you'd have blackmailed him yourself. You've got a lot of ideas, but no proof. Well, I have proof. I have proof of lots of things. Why do you think the last Lord Stapleford kept me on? I know more about that family than anyone. I've kept my notes down the years. Bided my time. You want it? You want all I've got?' Spittle clung to her lips. She was raving like a madwoman, so I made the only answer I could.

'Yes,' I said.

'You can have it. You can have it all if you find out what happened to my Sophy. I don't want stories. I want facts. If Richard Stapleford killed her then he must hang for it.'

Chapter Eleven

Confessing the Truth to Bertram

Mrs Wilson refused to say another word to us. No plea could elicit a determination of whether she had recognised her attacker. Her lost child was now all her concern. She had set out her terms for aiding us and we were forced to accept them.

Rory and I spoke little on the return journey to London. We were both tired and we had to rush for our train. As I sat in the carriage feeling the jolt of wheels against the track and listening to the sound of the chuffing engine the enormity of what we had done began to strike home. We had stolen our employer's vehicle, though it was now returned, and we had taken a day's absence without leave. And what did we have to show for it? The attack on Mrs Wilson was very real, but everything else was surmise and conjecture. I knew from bitter experience how Mr Bertram reacted to such. I stole a look at Rory's profile. His face was grimly set.

'Regrets?' I asked, the words scraping harshly in my throat.

His face softened slightly. 'Nay, lass. We did what we had to. What will come will come.'

'You didn't have to,' I said.

'Aye, well, I couldnae let you do it alone now,

161

could I?'

The joint burdens of guilt and responsibility settled heavily on my shoulders and by the time we reached London I felt their weight so badly I feared I would not be able to stand upright.

When we arrived back at the hotel it was past tea time, but before the dinner hour. The train journey had left me smutty and dirty as steam travel will and I did not feel equal to meeting Mr Bertram in my dishevelled state. I suggested to Rory that we left a message at the reception that we had returned and would await his convenience, with a suggestion that we would be happy to see him after dinner.

'Good idea,' said Rory. 'He's bound to be angry. But if he's angry and hungry then we have no chance of getting him to hear us out.'

'I could see him alone,' I said.

Rory shook his head. 'This is going to take both of us. It's not every day you tell a man he has an illegitimate sister.'

'A dead illegitimate sister,' I corrected. 'I only hope he believes us.'

One of the luxuries of staying in a hotel, no matter how small a room you have been given, is hot water on command. After I had soaked my weary body in its warmth I realised how very hungry I was. I rang up reception and asked them to send me up an omelette and salad. I asked if there was any message for me and was told not.

I had almost finished an omelette light and fluffy enough to have been worthy of Mrs Deighton when my door opened without a knock. Mr Bertram stood in the doorway, a bottle of wine and two glasses in his hand. I half-rose, but he waved me back to my seat. 'Don't trouble yourself, Euphemia. You obviously no longer work for me, so I have brought you a glass of wine to toast your new endeavours. Am I to wish you and Mr McLeod joy?'

I saw at once that this was not the first bottle he had opened this evening. 'No, there is nothing of that nature,' I said carefully. 'I do indeed hope to remain in your employ. I have matters of great importance to tell you. I am sorry I could not take you into my confidence before, but you were heavily engaged with poor Miss Wilton's funeral observations.'

Mr Bertram sat down opposite me. Although my room was more than adequate, having a small table and two chairs as well as the usual bedroom furniture, it suddenly seemed rather cramped. He placed the glasses down and poured wine sloppily from the open bottle into both. 'Where did a maid learn to talk like you?' he asked. 'Richard thinks you're a high-class courtesan who is exploring a new career option. I think he remains hopeful you will forsake your godly ways and return to your true nature. But I think you remain virginal. Am I right?'

'Good God, Mr Bertram! You cannot ask me questions like that!'

'Why?' said Bertram. He leaned over the table and I could see his eyes glittering from drink. 'Why can't I ask you indecent questions? You, who see fit to steal my automobile and run around the country with my brother's servants in a manner any man of good conscience would

163

find immoral.'

'We borrowed the vehicle,' I said, 'but I have done nothing of an immoral nature. I swear.' I pushed to the back of my mind how much I had enjoyed Rory's grasp on my hand. In the scheme of things I had to impart to Mr Bertram alone it seemed a small and distant thing.

'I always listen to you, don't I?' Mr Bertram said. 'Before you arrived on our doorstep my family was happy. My father was alive. Cousin George was alive. Our friends had never witnessed murder under our hospitality. My brother and sister and I were all companionable. My mother spoke to me. You know, Euphemia, since her retreat to Brighton my mother no longer communicates with me? She has expressed the opinion that I have fallen into low company that is leading me astray. She means you.'

'I am going to ring for some coffee,' I said as evenly as I could. I was furious, but I knew better than to give Mr Bertram the fight he was so clearly seeking. 'I have much to tell you and it would be better if you were sober.'

'I can hardly wait to hear it,' said Bertram lounging back in his chair. 'Your tales are worthy of a novel.'

'Oh, come,' I said with a flare of temper. 'They are never that bad.'

'Are you going to summon Rory McLeod to your rescue?'

I hesitated. I did dearly want Rory here to help me explain the situation, but I feared his presence would only inflame matters. 'No,' I said. 'I think we must first settle matters between us.'

'So what is going on this time, Euphemia?'

'I shall wait until you have drunk your coffee,' I said icily.

And I did. Though he gibed me with words and comments I do not now even care to remember. My father was never a heavy drinker although he had spoken to me of the evils of taking too much wine. He used to say it put an unhappy man at odds with himself and turned his malice outwards to destroy innocent targets. I clung to this memory rather than listen to the deluge of vile comments Mr Bertram uttered. I saw beyond his distress to a man who not only felt out of his depth, but was also grieving heavily for a woman who had died while in his care. If my position was uncomfortable his was doubly so.

I waited until he had finished his third cup. By this time he had begun to frown. I hoped this was a sign that he realised how very badly he had behaved.

'I am sorry about taking the automobile,' I said. 'I needed to visit an asylum in the country. Mr Edward had sent me the address as a place of interest although he did not say, or perhaps did not exactly know, why. He told me only that your father had been donating heavily to the place up until his death.'

'I thought you had disregarded my order about Edward,' said Bertram sulkily. 'But why would my father do such a thing?'

'It is a children's asylum and the lady who works there told us she had had the care of your father's niece, Sophy, until her removal to a London establishment.'

'What niece? All my cousins are male.'

'The asylum she was removed to was the one Miss Wilton wished to investigate.'

'What are you saying?'

'I am hoping the police have returned Beatrice's notebook to either you or her family.'

'I've been given nothing,' said Bertram. He mopped his head with his handkerchief. 'I may be making a leap here, but are you suggesting that this Sophy might be my father's child and that he placed her in an institution to hide her?'

I shook my head. 'She was what they call a "six months' child". Simple and affectionate, but unable to live in the real world.'

'But her mother?'

'Was Mrs Wilson, who until recently believed the girl had died at birth.'

'Good God! That my father could have been such a fiend!'

'It may be,' I said gently, 'that he mistakenly thought he was being kind letting her believe the child was gone.'

'Are you sure, Euphemia, that you are right about this?'

I noted for all the disagreements between us he did not consider that I might be lying or attempting to blackmail him. 'It all fits neatly into place,' I said. 'I think Beatrice suspected Sophy's existence and pushed the glass to see if she could get a reaction from Mrs Wilson. Of course, I can't know this, but I hope her notes will confirm this.'

'But however did she find out?'

'I don't know, but Mrs Wilson – that's who we travelled to see yesterday – does admit there was a child. She says she has a number of family papers that could resolve a number of mysteries we have touched upon and that she will give them up if we solve the mystery of what happened to Sophy.'

'But you know what happened to her,' said Bertram.

'I'm very sorry to tell you,' I said quietly, 'but your half-sister died recently.'

'How?'

I shook my head helplessly.

'Oh no,' said Bertram. 'You're not about to tell me that Mrs Wilson's attack, Miss Wilton's death and Sophy's death are all linked? You're not going to tell me you suspect...?'

'Murder,' I supplied. 'Yes, I'm rather afraid I am.'

It was at this point that Bertram agreed to summon Rory and we went over all the details again and again. I cannot say that we progressed matters except that we finally got Mr Bertram to admit that there was serious cause for concern and that it needed investigating.

'I can't condone what you did,' he said, 'but I appreciate you were both acting in the best interests of the family.' He fixed his attention on Rory. 'Euphemia and I have suspected my elder brother of more than one nefarious act, but I cannot imagine him killing or arranging to have killed, as he would have to have done, his own half-sister.'

'Is it more incredible than killing his own father?' I asked.

'There was never proof,' said Bertram defensively.

167

I dropped the point. Once, he had been certain of his brother's guilt, but that was in the heat of grief and passion for justice. The passage of time had tempered this and he was, like most men, keener to seek an easy resolution.

'You heard him arguing with Mrs Wilson on the evening of her attack,' said Bertram. 'Is it possible he didn't know? That the revelation Beatrice unleashed caught him by surprise? My father died suddenly. Perhaps he had intended to tell us, or at least Richard, about Sophy, but never did.'

'You mean Mrs Wilson thought he knew, but he didn't?' said Rory. 'Mrs Wilson said as much.'

Bertram nodded eagerly.

'With all respect, sir, wouldn't that have made him all the more likely to act?'

'But it doesn't make sense,' I said. 'She wouldn't be entitled to anything under his last will, would she?'

Bertram shook his head. 'If she hadn't been simple, perhaps, but no, nothing at all. The only claim she would have had on the family was a moral one. I admit Richard might have felt as an MP he would have had to settle money on her or Mrs Wilson, but he's rich enough for that not to matter.'

'But Beatrice wanted to write a story about it,' I said. 'And she had convinced you to help her.'

Bertram sank his head into his hands. 'I know. I know. I led her into danger. My wretched, wretched family.'

Rory coughed. 'Perhaps we should all retire to rest now, sir. It's been a long day and we have much to think about.'

'Yes,' I said. 'I think that would be wise. If you would be willing to request sight of Beatrice's notebook from the police or her family – whoever has it – it may make matters much clearer.'

'I need to think,' said Bertram. 'I hope at the end of all this I will have reason to feel grateful to you both. I do accept that you had the interests of justice at heart.'

And with this he walked unsteadily from the room.

'Och, these Staplefords,' said Rory. 'They make me regret I ever came south of the border. I'm away to my bed and you should do the same, lass. No doubt yon mannie will have a fine scheme by the morning.'

The way he said "fine" made it clear he thought it would be anything but. I could not but agree. I slept fitfully, worried about what the morning would bring.

I awoke to a brilliant day with a sky of quite breathtaking blue peeping through my curtains. Looking out the window I saw the people of the city going about their business briskly and with the liveliness that such an unexpected sunny day always engenders. It was a reminder to me that whatever fills our own hearts the world continues to turn. Only a few days ago Miss Wilton would have looked out at a similar tableau from her own room never dreaming that this would be the last building in which she would sleep and that she would never see her home again.

I was in a melancholy frame of mind as I made my way down to the breakfast hall. Bertram was already seated. I was unsure of the protocol now Beatrice was gone, but it was a public place and I was posing as a lady's companion, so I took my seat by him. Rory, of course, as a butler was not able to join us.

Mr Bertram cracked the top of his egg decisively. 'I have decided what our next step should be,' he said. 'You and I, Euphemia, will visit Dr Frank's asylum and enquire directly what happened to Sophy. I will say I have only recently become aware of her existence due to the sudden nature of my father's death and I wish to know what became of her.'

'It is a very direct course of action,' I said.

'We will leave a note at the reception saying where we have gone. You may also send word to Edward if you wish. I shall mention this if the situation seems to become at all threatening. You see, I have thought this through.'

'But if the asylum is in any way implicated in her death what makes you think that they will admit it?' I said. 'We have already met Dr Frank and he was fully aware of who you were. He showed not the slightest sign of defence or nervousness.'

'He didn't let us see around the asylum as Beatrice asked,' retorted Bertram.

'But I don't think they do that any more,' I said. 'He told us they have commissioners who inspect them and who can arrive at any time.'

Bertram sighed. 'You're very naive, Euphemia. A little money in the right places would ensure that the asylum always had notice of such visits. Clerks make very little money.'

'I cannot help but feel this is precipitous, sir.'

'Well, I am going after breakfast,' said Mr Bertram. 'You can either come with me or wait at the hotel. So far you and Rory have done all the investigating, but this is a family matter and I must attend to it personally.'

He had a stubborn set about his jaw that I recognised. It was the same expression he had used when he had repeatedly refused to listen to my warnings about White Orchards' cellar. 'I will come with you,' I said. 'Please give me a few minutes to prepare.'

I returned to my room and snatched up my coat. I then made my way to the front desk as quickly as I could. Mr Bertram was not in sight. With the help of my friend the concierge I obtained the number I needed from the operator. My hand shook as I held the telephone. After an interminable wait I was put through.

'Could I speak to Mrs Mason, please?'

'Can I say what it is about?' asked a polite female voice.

'I visited two days ago – about my daughter. She may be joining you. I'd rather not give my name.'

'Of course, ma'am.'

There were a few clicks and Mrs Mason's voice came on line. 'How can I help, my dear?'

'I'm struggling with my final decision,' I said. 'It really is the thought of what happens next. When she is grown. I wondered if it might be possible to speak to one of your charges who had moved on to the next stage.'

'I see,' said Mrs Mason. 'There is an issue of confidentiality.'

171

'Of course, but you mentioned someone – Amy, was it? Who was a friend of Sophy's?'

'Yes, I did, didn't I?'

'I wondered if she is still at the same asylum that Sophy attended.'

'I have not heard she has moved,' said Mrs Mason with admirable discretion.

'Although I did wonder if she might be too upset to see me. Was what happened to Sophy recent?'

There was an intake of breath at the other end of the phone.

'The family doesn't talk about it,' I said quickly. 'In the same way I imagine they will not talk about my daughter when her time comes.' I managed a little half-sob.

'It's kind of you to consider Alice's feelings. Alice, not Amy. I don't know how she will take it. Sometimes these simple souls accept matters of life and death much more easily than we do.'

'So it was recent.' I said.

'Very,' said Mrs Mason. 'I do not wish to be unsympathetic, but I feel I have already said more than I should. I give you my word that should you decide to place your daughter with us I will ensure she has the very best care and attention.'

'I have no doubt of that,' I said sincerely. 'Thank you.'

I rang off and went to sit in one of the foyer chairs awaiting Bertram. I felt incredibly guilty, but at least now I had a plan. It was a much better one than Mr Bertram had suggested, but it was also far, far more dangerous.

172

Chapter Twelve

Meeting Alice

The main reason my plan was so dangerous was that I could tell no one about it. I greeted Mr Bertram with a guarded smile and listened respectfully to all his ideas as we set forth in the hired carriage. These were rambling and inconclusive. They centred around finding any excuse for his brother not to be involved. When he paused I did not point out any of the obvious flaws, but instead asked, 'Did you not wish Rory to accompany us?'

Bertram frowned. 'I thought it would be easier to seek an audience if it was the same party as those who he had met before. I intend to tell him about Beatrice's death and see if he reacts.'

'If he reads the newspapers he will surely know about it,' I said.

'But not that we suspect murder!' retorted Bertram. 'Nor that we know there was another doctor involved!'

'But we don't have any proof of that either.' I could not prevent a wailing note from entering my voice.

'I shall face him man to man,' said Bertram. 'You wouldn't understand how these things work, Euphemia, but I assure you I will know if he is guilty of aiding in Beatrice's demise.'

At this point I chose to smile politely and nod.

If I argued further he would see how little I thought of his plan and wonder why I had come. I regretted Rory was not with us. He would surely have seen the danger of confronting a potential accomplice to nefarious activities on his own ground armed only with a moral compass. One's sense of morality, no matter how acute, is I have sadly learned no match for cold steel or indeed ruthless determination. I could not help wishing that this matter had been of national interest and we had had someone with the skills and flexible outlook of one such as Mr Fitzroy to accompany us.

I had many ideas of what we might find at the asylum. The most likely discovery I thought we would make was some indication that Richard Stapleford had been in communication with them recently and before Sophy's death. I thought it unlikely that we would be able to link them with the doctor Beatrice had told Bertram had visited her before the arrival of the hotel doctor. I was fairly confident in my mind that this first doctor had been the product of Beatrice's desire to ease Bertram's worries. I would be more than content should all roads lead to Lord Richard, but I knew by now that friends in high places and money could hide many actions. I also thought that Bertram was liable to only find more suspicion rather than proof. The best I felt that could be gained from his actions was a cat among the pigeons effect with someone somewhere making a mistake such as sending an ill-advised communication. It seemed a very outside chance. Even my own plan had little chance of success. But what else could we do? Never could I have imagined what we were to find.

From the outside the asylum had not changed since the three of us were here a few days before. Having seen the countryside estate style of the children's asylum I could now see that in reality this was a small affair. It was also extremely well kept and I suspected full of patients from the better classes of society. Mr Bertram marched up to the door and rang the bell. I followed more slowly in his wake. The same woman we had seen before opened the door to us. Mr Bertram demanded to see Dr Frank. She demurred. Mr Bertram began to raise his voice. A large male attendant appeared behind the woman. I won't go as far to say his shoulders were wider than the door, but he was well muscled. Mr Bertram refused to back down. When I feared things might go as far as to become physical I placed a restraining hand on Bertram's arm.

'Come away,' I said clearly and coldly. 'I shall return to the commissioners and tell them we were refused entry. They can come down and see for themselves.'

My words acted as a cold shower on the scene. Mr Bertram opened his mouth to utter what I felt certain would be a stinging reprimand, when the woman at the door said, 'I am so sorry, sir. I didn't understand you had come with the commissioners' blessing. You should have said. Of course Dr Frank will make himself available for you. I didn't lie when I said he was very busy today, so I am afraid you may have to wait some little while in his office. It should be comfortable enough and it is for your own safety.'

'Do you have dangerous inmates here?' asked Bertram.

'Indeed we do, sir,' growled the man. 'That is why we has to be most unencouraging of visitors. But like Mrs Turner says if you have the commissioners' ear it is quite a different matter.'

I inwardly prayed Bertram would have the sense not to correct their assumption. He did give me a strange look, but allowed himself to be led inside. Once through the door we were led along the same set of corridors as before and into Dr Frank's office. Our male escort peeled away at the outset, but I was alarmed to see that Mrs Turner also took a seat in the office. 'John will tell him you are here,' she said.

'Please don't let us detain you from your duties,' said Bertram.

'I couldn't possibly leave you alone,' said Mrs Turner with a smile that had several implications. We were still suspected.

I had hoped to search the good doctor's desk for patient records and, from the disappointed air that hung around Bertram, I believe he had had the same thought. I rose from my seat, coughed slightly and began to pace the room. I passed by the picture of the asylum I had seen during my last visit and managed to ascertain that everything was how I remembered. I paced a little longer, growing obviously more agitated.

'Euphemia, is there something wrong?' The genuine concern in Bertram's voice was my cue to collapse to the floor. I have only once fainted in my life and had no real idea how to do it again, so

I closed my eyes and threw myself down. In doing so I hit my poor head hard on the floor. For a moment I was overcome by dizziness and nausea. Mr Bertram helped me into a chair. I croaked something about water and Mrs Turner, who was the one I was most worried about fooling, appeared both convinced and concerned. She held my wrist in a professional manner and pronounced my pulse was fluttery.

'She suffered a bad concussion a few days ago,' said Mr Bertram. 'I should never have brought her to London.'

'Indeed not, sir,' said Mrs Turner. 'I wouldn't be surprised if that faint hasn't brought it all back again. This is no place for a young woman of sensibility and refinement.'

'She's...' began Mr Bertram and then with rare sense stopped.

'I think you should take her right home, sir, if you don't mind me being so bold...'

'I think you might be right,' said Mr Bertram with what I felt was a woeful lack of insight.

'Water,' I whispered throatily.

'Of course, duck,' said Mrs Turner. 'You rest there a moment. I'll be right back.'

The moment the door closed behind her I rose shakily to my feet.

'Euphemia, you must rest.'

'Rubbish,' I said smoothing down my dress. 'I did that on purpose.' I put up a hand to rub my head. 'I do wish I had not misjudged the edge of the rug, but it can't be helped. My vision appears to have returned to normal.' I steadied myself with a hand on the back of the chair. 'If she

177

returns before I do you must say I felt the need for some air.'

'What? How? Why?' babbled Bertram.

'I am going to find Sophy's friend Alice,' I said. 'I have no more time to debate this.' I made my way across the room, but Bertram caught me by the wrist.

'I'll come with you,' said Bertram. Sometimes he clearly displayed more courage than sense.

'She will be in the women's quarters,' I explained. 'You would be immediately noticed. With luck I will be able to slip in. My dress is quite plain and I may well be mistaken for an inmate.'

'No, Euphemia. You can't. They will know everyone in here. Besides you have no idea of where to go!'

I pulled my arm free and pointed to the map on the wall I had taken pains to study earlier.

'You'll never find her,' cried Bertram. 'You don't even know what she looks like!'

'Make my excuses as best you can,' I said and slipped out the door.

For a moment I feared he would follow me or open the door and cry out, but he did not. The corridor I was in was quiet and empty. My heart beat fast in my chest and I almost wished Bertram had managed to stop me. I took a deep breath and headed off in the general direction where I expected the women's quarters to be. The map I had studied had only shown the outline of the buildings, so I headed in what I hoped was an easterly direction.

Unfortunately I soon found myself at a cross

junction. The passage behind me had been wood panelled. The three ways forward were white with wooden doors set at intervals down the sides. The asylum had suddenly taken on much more of the form of a hospital. I chose the way that seemed most easterly and continued on. A low moan issued from behind one of the doors I passed and I felt the hairs rise on my neck. I suddenly remembered Mrs Turner's warning that the asylum harboured dangerous inmates. I had taken this as a deterrent for visitors rather than the truth, but now I wondered. I quickened my pace.

Ahead of me stretched a series of doors on either side. The passage ended in a door and I hurried towards it not caring what lay on the other side. This was a mistake. My boots rang against the hard floor. Suddenly there were noises coming from behind several of the doors. Then came a loud bang. I stopped, turning around. The noise came again and I saw one door shake. Something heavy was being thrown against it by an inmate. It did not give way, but I was unconvinced how heavy an assault it would take. My mind conjured hideous possibilities of whom or what lay on the other side. I took to my heels and fled the length of the corridor not caring if I ran straight into Mrs Turner or one of the other staff. In fact, I rather hoped I would.

I slammed hard against the exit only considering on impact that it might not open, but fortune favoured me and the door gave. Suddenly I was outside in the bright sunlight. I put up a hand to shade my eyes and looked about me. It was a lawned garden. I cast my mind back to the map and realised I wasn't as far from my destination as I feared.

This area had been labelled the formal garden. Ahead of me lay two long buildings: one for men and one for women. Behind these, I recalled lay the work buildings, the laundry, the water tower, the refectory and a few other unnamed buildings that doubtless had equally utilitarian purposes.

The garden was lovely. There were meandering paths that ended in small follies and summer-houses. A maze of low hedges between the flowerbeds gave the illusion of privacy, but would allow an attendant to clearly see any pedestrians. I saw two walkers in the distance approaching a small folly. They had not yet seen me, but it was only a matter of time. There was nowhere for me to hide. I did the only thing I could and walked purposefully forward towards the building I was almost certain housed the women.

I kept my head up and my eyes forward. I was within 20 steps of the building when a bell rang and two doors in its side opened. Women in white dresses poured out. They were all ages from youthful to those tottering with the support of canes. Some of them were neatly kempt and others had the wild, wind-blown hair that the popular papers associate with the insane. Of course, Dr Frank had said that they believed in healthy exercise for all the inmates. This must be their daily constitution. At least I could be fairly certain none of those present would be violent.

However, I knew there must be attendants. I would not have long. I started to look around for anyone who could be Alice. I knew Mrs Wilson had worked for the late Lord Stapleford prior to his first marriage. I didn't know when Sophy had been born, but it seemed logical that any dalliance must have occurred before his marriage in order for him to keep it secret from the rest of the family. Alice was of age with Sophy, so I began to search for any woman who looked slightly older than Richard.

It was very difficult to tell. I approached one woman and asked gently if she was Alice. Pale blue eyes stared into mine. Tentatively she put out a hand and touched my hair. 'Is it you, Margaret?' she asked.

'No, I'm afraid not,' I said. 'I'm a friend of Sophy's. I'm looking for her friend Alice.'

'Sophy's gone,' said the woman. 'They took her away in the night.'

'Who took her?' I asked, a cold shiver creeping down my back.

'Why, the dead ones,' said the woman. 'They come at night and take their own.' She leaned in closer. Her breath was strangely sickly and sweet 'They have no faces.'

'Of course,' I said retreating, but the woman still had hold of my hair. She held hard. 'Guard your virtue,' she warned in a low, gravelly voice. 'You're a fair one. They all get taken. All of them. I've been here since I was a girl and I've seen them all go. No safety for the pretty ones. Like my father said, beauty is a curse. You're cursed. Cursed to hell.'

The words were uttered without anger. It made them all the more chilling. Gently I disentangled her fingers from my hair and stepped away. As I would with a feral animal I kept my eyes on her until I was clear then turned quickly and walked away without looking back.

All at once I desperately wanted my father. I wanted him to explain to me why God could be so cruel to cripple minds inside healthy bodies.

I made my way towards one of the summer-houses. This had been a foolish plan. I should seek out an attendant, explain I had been taken ill and hopefully someone would escort me back to Dr Frank's office.

Inside I found an attendant in a blue dress seated on a bench. She looked up as I entered and I saw she had been crying. 'Can I help?' I said without thinking.

'Help?' asked the woman. Her voice was light and clear. 'I don't think anyone can help me now.'

'Oh, I'm sure that's not the case,' I said sitting down next to her. 'There is always something to be done.' I confess that I meant this merely as a platitude. I was hoping to enlist her support to return to the main building without fuss.

'I'm going the same way as Sophy,' said the attendant. 'Poor Sophy.'

'Sophy?' I exclaimed.

'We came up together,' said the woman. 'She was a simple soul, but she had a lovely nature. She could do most tasks if it was explained clearly. She trusted everyone. Never any trouble.'

'What happened to her?' I asked.

'She died.'

'But how?'

'At night. The doctors came into the ward in the morning in gowns and masks and took her

182

away. She looked like she was asleep. They said she had caught something very bad and it had made her die.'

'Caught something very bad?' I echoed blankly. 'Couldn't they be more specific?'

'Possibly, but not to me. Poor Sophy. She and I came here together.'

'You're Alice?' I asked. 'I thought you worked here. You don't seem...'

'Mad?' said Alice. 'I have fits.' She saw my expression. 'Shaking fits. I'm not violent or anything like that, but it makes people uncomfortable. And if I'm not with someone I can hurt myself by accident.'

'I see,' I said looking around for her attendant.

'They don't bother with me now,' said Alice. 'Not since I started having the dreams too.'

'The dreams?'

'They came to Sophy before she died, so I know I'm going to die too.'

'Dreams can't kill you,' I said kindly.

'Sophy's dreams did. She dreamt the masked man came for her every night. He made her drink a medicine and then everything got strange and confused and the world got all whirling and wobbly. I didn't believe her. I thought she was making it up. She liked to make up stories. But now I have the dreams too.'

'She obviously told you the dreams very clearly and you are remembering them. It's horrible when someone you care for dies. You think there should have been something you could do for her, but there wasn't. She got ill and she died. It's very sad, but it wasn't the dreams.'

183

'But I'm the same as her,' cried Alice placing her hand on her stomach. 'They haven't noticed yet, because it's not very big, but I can see it. I'm getting fat just like Sophy did. She said it felt like things were moving inside her. I don't want that to happen to me. I don't want to be killed by something eating my insides.'

Very gently I reached out and touched Alice's stomach. There was no mistaking her condition. I felt tears sting my eyes. 'My dear, you're not being devoured from within, I promise you. You're going to have a baby.'

Chapter Thirteen

Adventure at the Asylum

The ramifications of Alice's condition shook me to the core. There was only one interpretation that could be placed upon her and Sophy's dreams. What was clear was that I could not leave her here.

'You need to come with me,' I said rising. 'I will help you, but we must go at once.'

'We're not allowed to leave the gardens until the next bell sounds,' said Alice.

Confusion was written all over her face.

'But you're not safe here!'

Alice's face crumpled. 'I don't understand. This is my home.'

Behind her, through the lattice of the

summerhouse wall, I saw the unmistakable figure of Mrs Turner. At her side was the larger, now more menacing figure of John.

'Please,' I begged. 'You need to come with me.'

Alice shook her head. Mrs Turner and John were growing closer. I wracked my brains. Why couldn't Alice understand? She wasn't insane by her own admission, but as I looked into her frightened eyes I realised that I had under-estimated the impact of spending her entire life in an institution. She was as ignorant of the outside world as she was of what was happening to her own body. It struck me now she had not reacted to my announcement that she was having a child. My pronouncement had made no sense to her. She was as naive as a child.

I took her hand gently. 'Why don't we go and see Dr Frank and let him sort this out?' I said. 'You know Dr Frank, don't you?'

Her face lit up. 'Oh yes! He's always nice to me. He is going to make me well.'

'Come on then,' I said pulling her to her feet. 'Let's go and see him now and he can make everything better. That's what doctors do, isn't it?'

Her hand slid into mine and she smiled happily. All her cares were suddenly vanished. She might not be simple, but her mind clearly worked as trustingly as a child's. No wonder she and the simple Sophy had been friends. But how was I to get her past Mrs Turner and John? I dismissed ideas of playing hide and seek. She might be childlike, but she wasn't a child and she was far from incapable of rational thought. I had to get her away without arousing any more fears or suspicions.

I peered around the edge of the summerhouse door. Mrs Turner was hurrying off up the path away from us. If only I could persuade Alice to walk directly to the entrance to the treatment corridor I was confident I could find my way back to Bertram. I prayed he hadn't gone to find me. Everything depended on reaching his protection as soon as possible.

'Alice, we'll have to go quickly,' I said. 'You'll want to be back for when the bell goes to return to your room, won't you?'

'I go to work in the laundry next.'

'Well, the laundry then,' I said trying to stay calm and fighting a rising panic. As I watched John at Mrs Turner's side I wondered if he was the man molesting the women and what he might do to me if he caught me alone out here. Would Mrs Turner help me? How many of the staff were involved in these atrocities? It struck me as likely that the male attendants, who must often be called in to subdue difficult situations, were most likely to be tempted. 'We'll have to go directly to Dr Frank. Through that door over there.'

Alice began to tremble. 'That's the treatment row. I don't need treatment. I haven't had a fit in weeks. I don't need it. I don't need it!' Her voice rose in panic.

'You won't have any,' I promised desperately. 'It's the shortest way to Dr Frank.'

'I don't need treatment,' repeated Alice, wild eyed.

'You won't have any,' I said. 'You'll be with me.

I'll look after you.'

These last four words had a remarkable effect. Alice stopped shaking and looked directly at me. 'You promise?'

'I promise,' I said. 'Come on.'

I led her quickly across the garden. I did as I had done before and kept my head up and my eyes forward. I walked as if I had every right to be here and every right to lead Alice from this place. It is true that I felt I had a moral right to do as I did and this lent me courage.

We were almost at the door when I heard John's voice call out. 'That's her!' I clenched Alice's hand in a tight grip and plunged through the door. 'Run!' I said. 'Dr Frank only has a few minutes to see us.'

Alice laughed. 'This is fun,' she said.

I pelted along the corridor. Our passing caused the inmates of the treatment cells to stir again. There were groans and moans the like of which I hope never to hear again. Alice's laughter was chilling and I wondered if she was as sane as she protested.

We reached the junction. I spun on the spot, twirling Alice round behind me. She thought this was a great game. Our exit was not hard to spot. It was the only panelled corridor. I set off again, dragging Alice, who was now protesting she felt dizzy. Behind us I heard running footsteps and knew I only had moments to reach the office. Was it the third or the fourth door along? I couldn't remember.

I chose at random and burst in on a flabbergasted Bertram and startled Dr Frank, who both shot to their feet. Hard on my heels came Mrs Turner and John. I pulled Alice with me into the centre of the room. I stood there panting, looking round at the unfriendly faces. For a few moments no one said anything. Bertram broke the silence.

'Euphemia, are you feeling better?' he said.

'This woman is pregnant,' I said. 'Tell me how that can happen in your asylum, Dr Frank?' I turned to face John. 'Or should I ask you? A male attendant in an institution full of helpless women! What did you give them? A sleeping draught? What evil!'

'She fainted earlier, Dr Frank,' said Mrs Turner. 'Hit her head on the floor. She suffered a bad concussion earlier in the week as well.'

'That might explain much,' said Dr Frank in a professionally calm voice. 'Come and sit down, Miss St John. Let me have a look at you.'

'Bertram,' I exclaimed. 'Don't you see what is going on here?'

'I'm sure Euphemia has a rational explanation, Dr Frank,' said Bertram.

'This is Alice, Bertram. Sophy's friend. She and Sophy had the same dreams. They were being drugged. Then men came to them. She doesn't understand what happened. She thinks, like Sophy thought, that she is being eaten by something from the inside, but it's a baby.'

'My dear Miss St John, I assure you that no woman in this institution has ever conceived a child,' said Dr Frank.

'Except Mrs Hutchins,' said Mrs Turner, 'but she is married and on staff.'

'Of course, you must have seen her in the

188

corridor,' said Dr Frank. 'It must have set off this delusion. Do sit down. I assure you this sort of thing is not uncommon after a blow to the head. It will pass in time.'

'Perhaps I should fetch something,' said Mrs Turner.

'I think that would be a good idea,' said Dr Frank. 'If you could take Alice back to her room, John.'

'Of course, doctor,' said John. 'Come with me please, Alice.'

'No, wait!' I cried.

John approached Alice and took her arm. Mrs Turner crossed to a cabinet in the corner and, taking a key from the chain at her waist, unlocked it. 'A draught, doctor?'

'Something a little swifter, I think,' said Dr Frank.

Mrs Turner took out a small bottle and began to fill a syringe. Dr Frank came towards me. I backed away and stumbled into a chair. 'There,' he said. 'Isn't it better to be sitting down?'

Bertram still stood. 'Don't let him harm me,' I shouted to him. 'We must help Alice and her baby.'

Bertram spread his hands helplessly.

'You can't let them do this to me!'

'I should never have brought you to London,' said Bertram. 'It has been too much.'

'You have to believe me!' I cried. John was leading Alice from the room. 'Alice,' I begged. 'You have to tell them what happened to you! You have to tell Dr Frank.'

'It's all right, Alice,' said Dr Frank. 'You're not

189

in any trouble. Our visitor is a little confused. John will take you back to your room. I'll see you later.'

'Alice, tell them about what is inside you!' I pleaded.

'Time to go, Alice,' said John. He began to pull her towards the door. Alice turned back and looked at me. Her face expressed doubt and fear. My attention was all on her and so I didn't see Mrs Turner until she had my arm in a vice-like grip. 'Now, stay still, like a good girl,' she said, 'and this won't hurt a bit.' The syringe hovered above my skin.

'Tell them what happened to Sophy!' But Alice ignored my pleas and walked placidly towards the door with John. 'Don't let her give me treatment!' I shouted. Every muscle in Alice's back went rigid. John pulled on her arm. 'Come on, Alice,' he urged, but she was immoveable. I jerked my arm away from Mrs Turner. She was leaning over me, so I couldn't rise.

'I might need a little help, Dr Frank,' she said.

Dr Frank placed a hand on Bertram's shoulder. 'I realise this is all very unpleasant, but it is for the best. Miss St John isn't in her right mind. She doesn't know what is best of her.'

'Bertram, please!'

'You need to be brave, Mr Stapleford. Miss St John needs our help. You must trust me.'

'No,' I panted, jerking sideways in my chair, as Mrs Turner grabbed for me again. 'Don't trust him.'

'You are overwrought,' said Bertram averting his face.

'Alice!' I shouted. 'They're going to give me treatment!'

I had heard of the strength of the mad, but I had never seen it. My words caused a greater effect than I could have imagined. Alice tore herself from John's grip, pushing him hard to the ground at the same time. She uttered a harsh cry and threw herself at Mrs Turner. The nurse was knocked to the ground. They went down together, turning over and over, until Mrs Turner plunged the needle into Alice and she went limp.

Mrs Turner sat up and straightened her dress. 'I'll fetch another one, doctor,' she said in a breathless voice. She rose and went towards the cabinet.

I flew from my chair. 'My God! What have you done? The baby!' I rolled poor lifeless Alice onto her back.

'Now, Euphemia, don't interfere,' began Bertram, but his voice trailed off as Alice's loose clothes now draped around her fallen form clearly outlined a swollen belly.

'She has a tumour,' said Dr Frank.

'Then shouldn't she be in a hospital?' said Bertram.

'It's terminal,' said Dr Frank. 'There is nothing to be done. We have tried to keep it from her.'

'The same terminal condition that took Sophy's life!' I exclaimed. 'A pregnancy that has to be concealed! You know about this! I thought it had to be your staff without your knowledge, but you're involved!'

'What did Sophy die from?' asked Bertram.

'A myocardial infarction. A heart attack in lay-

191

man's terms. It's written on her death certificate.'

'Which you doubtless wrote,' I said. 'Was it you or John that visited Miss Wilton and helped her to the same condition?'

'The other doctor,' said Bertram in a voice of horror.

'My dear Mr Stapleford, don't let this poor deluded young woman convince you of her fantasies. I think perhaps you should leave. Miss St John's condition is far worse than I originally thought. I think it best she be admitted.'

'You can't do that!' I cried.

'Does she have family in town?' Dr Frank asked Bertram. 'If not would you be willing to vouch for her. I think the sooner she gets treatment the greater the chance of recovery. That original blow to the head must have been far worse than anyone thought. Did she see a London doctor?'

'No, our family man.'

'A good man, I have no doubt, but sometimes it needs a specialist to detect these things. Has she been prone to flights of fantasy before?'

'Bertram,' I said feeling tears spring to my eyes. 'You know me. You know I'm not mad.' I could not believe he was not defending me.

'Miss St John has a lively mind and quick intelligence,' said Bertram.

'That can make this sort of injury all the worse,' said Dr Frank.

'Bertram, you can see Alice is pregnant.'

'What you suggest is unthinkable, Euphemia. Alice has a tumour.'

'You can't commit me!'

Bertram shook his head. 'No, I can't. I think it

192

would be best if I took Euphemia away at once. I will see she gets the proper care.' He held out his hand to me. I took it.

'We can't leave her,' I said. 'I promised we'd help.'

'Thank you for all your help, Dr Frank. I cannot tell you what a relief it is to understand what happened to Sophy and that the short life she had was a pleasant one. You will understand it was a shock to discover she existed. I think it best that we leave now.'

John moved in front of the door, barring our exit.

'I am afraid I must insist you leave Miss St John in our care,' said Dr Frank. 'It is for her own good.'

'I don't agree,' said Bertram with all his old stubbornness. 'She is in my care.'

'As a doctor I can supersede that authority.'

'I feel certain you will not,' said Bertram belligerently.

'I have no choice,' said Dr Frank. 'It is in her best interests. Please stand aside.'

'Bertram, if you leave me here I will never be free,' I said clutching his arm. 'I know too much. They will make out I am mad. I will be committed for life.'

Mrs Turner had filled another syringe. 'Now, my dear,' she said smoothly. 'This will all go a lot easier if you don't resist.'

'I will not allow this,' said Bertram, placing himself between Mrs Turner and myself.

I opened my mouth to thank him, but before the words were past my lips John grabbed him in a practised arm-lock. 'Unhand me!' cried Bertram.

'I do regret this,' said Dr Frank. 'But family can be the last to see the problem.'

'I'm not family,' shouted Bertram. 'She's my housekeeper. Let me go. This is outrageous.'

'Ah,' said Dr Frank, 'and yet she calls you by your Christian name? Perhaps it is not surprising she imagines the result of fornication in other women. We have a term for this. It is called projection.'

'You villain,' I cried. 'You'll never get away with this!'

Mrs Turner's needle punctured my skin. The pain was sharp and hot. Bertram struggled to free himself from John's grip. The nurse pushed the plunger and the drug flooded into me.

'No!' I cried. The room began to swim before my eyes. 'No! Help! Help!'

My legs gave beneath me. I knew I was lost. In the distance I heard the sound of running feet. More attendants. What would happen to Bertram? My eyelids felt like lead. I felt myself slipping away. I offered up a confused but earnest prayer for help.

The last thing I saw was the door shattering into pieces as Rory burst through it. All the colours were too bright. I could no longer tell if this was real or a dream. I heard myself utter a long sigh. My mind slipped down into darkness.

Epilogue

When I came to I was in my own bed back in the hotel. My head throbbed alarmingly.

'Euphemia, can you ever forgive me?' Bertram's voice was both uncomfortably loud and seemed to come from a great distance at the same time.

'Not if she's any sense.' Rory's Scottish burr had never been so strong. 'What were ye thinking of, man, to take her into such danger?'

'I had no idea what she would try and do!' said Bertram.

'And how long have ye known the wench?' retorted Rory. 'Of course she had some plan up her sleeve.'

'I could not have imagined,' protested Bertram.

'Where's Alice?' I asked.

'She's in hospital,' said Rory. 'The doctors say she'll be fine and the bairn too.'

'I was right,' I exclaimed.

'Aye, you were. Though how you worked it all out is beyond me.'

'I didn't,' I confessed. 'My plan was to find Alice and talk to her about Sophy. I never imagined what was going on there.'

'Of course not,' said Bertram. 'It's beyond imagining. Dr Frank was a highly respected doctor.'

'He killed her, didn't he?' I said sadly. 'Sophy?'

'I don't know if we will ever know,' said Bertram. 'But he will never have charge of any

195

patient again.'

'I hope they send him to an asylum for the criminally insane,' said Rory. 'I hear they are terrible places and far less than he deserves.'

'How did you know to rescue us?'

'I told you I would leave word of where we have gone,' said Bertram testily.

'But did you overpower them all yourself?'

Bertram snorted. Rory laughed. 'No, lass. I called in a favour from Mr Edward. It seemed to me he could get things moving faster than your regular police service. It turns out he'd been looking for an excuse to raid the place for some time. He was more than happy to be of service.'

'We must let Mrs Wilson know what happened to Sophy.'

'All in good time,' said Bertram in an oddly gentle voice.

'What's happened?' I asked.

'The doctor said you should rest, Euphemia,' said Bertram. 'We can discuss all this in the morning.'

Panic shot through me. 'What's happened?' I demanded.

'Word came while you were away,' said Rory. 'She died of her injuries.'

'But she was recovering when we saw her!'

Rory laid a hand on my arm. 'Oh, lass, don't go making a mystery where there is none. She was seriously ill. The doctors said she could have gone at any time.'

There was a knock at the door. 'That will be my brother,' he said. 'I'll tell him you need to rest.'

'Lord Stapleford is here?'

'He came for the funeral,' said Bertram. 'Richenda and Tipton too.'

The door opened slightly. Lord Richard looked in. 'I wonder if I might have a word with our heroine,' he said.

'I'm not sure that's a good idea,' said Bertram. 'She's been through a lot.'

'Oh, I think Euphemia will want to hear what I have to say,' said Lord Richard. 'I have some good news for her.'

'What is it?' I asked.

'In private if you please, gentlemen.'

Rory and Bertram exchanged worried glances.

'It's all right,' I said.

'We'll be outside,' Rory whispered meaningfully as he passed me.

Lord Richard shut the door behind them. He pulled up a chair and sat down by my bed. 'You do involve yourself in the most extraordinary adventures.'

'It's not intentional,' I said.

Lord Richard laughed. 'Since you arrived at Stapleford Hall life has been so much more, er, enlivened. When you left for White Orchards the life seemed to go out of the place.'

It was a pretty sentiment, but behind the words I heard an acknowledgement of the battles we had fought.

'I do feel I left with my work undone,' I said.

'Quite,' said Lord Richard. 'And you know, somehow, Euphemia, I feel so much more secure when you're working for my household. Bertram has been very lax as an employer dragging you all around London and leading you into such awful situations.'

'I seem to remember a few awful situations back at Stapleford Hall,' I said.

Lord Richard smiled. 'Ah, but all that is in the past, isn't it? You will be pleased to hear I have strengthened the locks and added bolts to the windows. I doubt any intruder will ever again force his way into my home.'

'I'm sure everyone will feel safer for it,' I said evenly. 'Though there are often more dangers within a home than people generally imagine.'

'Indeed. I think we agree it is always better to keep one's eye on things personally?'

'Certainly.'

'Then you will understand why I feel it is the best course of action to offer you the now sadly vacant position of housekeeper at Stapleford Hall.'

I gasped. Stapleford Hall was more than five times the size of White Orchards. It was a substantial estate. It had been my dream on entering service to rise to the position of housekeeper at Stapleford Hall. I had foolishly promised my mother that I would quickly gain such a position, but I never imagined I would be offered it as the result of murder and unexplained deaths. It was on the tip of my tongue to refuse, but then I remembered Mrs Wilson saying she had papers on the family – papers that would incriminate them. Where would she have kept them but at the hall itself? I did not believe she had had any other home since her girlhood. If I was living under his roof I could not only watch Lord Stapleford, but search for Mrs Wilson's papers. My head throbbed painfully. I closed my eyes. I had fought many battles against Lord Richard and I had never won. Did I want to enter the lion's den once more?

'I am grateful to you for finding Sophy,' said Lord Richard. 'After that séance of Richenda's Mrs Wilson came to me accusing me of pushing the glass. I had no idea what the woman was talking about. My father had taken that secret to his grave. Strange to think I had a half-sibling I never knew anything about. Now, if her child had been born, it would have caused a lot of trouble. I never imagined it of my father, but then do we ever really know anyone?'

'What do you mean? How would her child have caused trouble?'

'My father's will leaves the estate to the first of his children who has a son.'

'But Bert-Mr Stapleford said it had to be a legitimate child.'

'He must have misunderstood me,' said Lord Richard. 'How odd. I thought I had been most clear on that point.'

'I see,' I said. 'So things have worked out very well for you.'

'And they could work out well for you too, Euphemia,' said Lord Richard. 'Really, I am not the ogre you think. Why I've even brought you flowers.' He turned and called behind him, 'Baggy! Bring them in!'

The door opened once more and Baggy Tipton came in carrying a huge bouquet. 'Richenda sends her regards,' he said. 'We all think you were very brave.'

'Thank you,' I stammered. As he laid the flowers on the bed he smiled at me. A cold chill washed over me. His eyes were bright blue; the same colour as my attacker.

I looked past Tipton and saw Lord Richard was watching me closely. 'Thank you,' I said. 'It is very kind of you both. And yes, Lord Richard, I would be delighted to accept your offer.'

'I'll send in my brother and you can give him your notice,' said Lord Richard. 'I'll ensure he doesn't make a fuss.'

They left. Bertram and Rory practically fell over each other to re-enter the room.

'He's offered me Mrs Wilson's situation,' I said at once. 'And I have accepted.'

'You can't!' said Bertram. 'I need you.'

'I have no idea if Lord Richard had any part in what happened to Sophy, but I am sure Tipton was the man who attacked Mrs Wilson and me.'

'Are you saying Lord Richard made him?' asked Rory.

'It seems the first male child of any of the late Lord Stapleford's children, legitimate or otherwise, will inherit Stapleford Hall,' I said.

'He wanted to shut her up,' said Rory.

'She said she had papers at the hall,' I said.

'I can look for them,' said Rory. 'There's no need to put yourself in harm's way.'

'But don't you see, if he suspects I know about Tipton then I'll never be safe. Sophy wasn't safe in the asylum and Miss Wilton wasn't safe here.'

'Beatrice died a natural death,' said Bertram.

'If she did,' I responded, 'why did no one ever find her notebooks? All her notes on her

200

investigation have vanished, haven't they?'

Bertram looked uncomfortable. 'I expect they will turn up. But I agree you mustn't return to Stapleford Hall. I don't know the extent of my brother's villainy, but I would fear for your safety.'

'I don't have a choice,' I said. 'Lord Richard is a powerful man. If I run he will find me. If I show no fear he will never be sure how much I know.'

'There has to be another option,' said Rory.

'There is,' said Bertram. He took a deep breath. 'After everything you've done for me and my family, Euphemia – after everything you've done in the name of justice and honour – it's my duty to protect you from my brother.' Then to my astonishment he went down on one knee. 'Euphemia, you are an incredible, brave and intelligent young woman. I admire you enormously. Marry me! As my wife you'll be safe. I'll keep you safe.'

'You!' said Rory. 'Man, you let her get stuck by a needle by yon mad doctor and his cronies.'

'So what do you suggest she should do,' asked Bertram waspishly.

'Why, marry me, of course,' said Rory. 'Well, lass, will ye have me?'

This Large Print Book for the partially sighted, who cannot read normal print, is published under the auspices of

THE ULVERSCROFT FOUNDATION

THE ULVERSCROFT FOUNDATION

... we hope that you have enjoyed this Large Print Book. Please think for a moment about those people who have worse eyesight problems than you ... and are unable to even read or enjoy Large Print, without great difficulty.

You can help them by sending a donation, large or small to:

**The Ulverscroft Foundation,
1, The Green, Bradgate Road,
Anstey, Leicestershire, LE7 7FU,
England.**
or request a copy of our brochure for more details.

The Foundation will use all your help to assist those people who are handicapped by various sight problems and need special attention.

Thank you very much for your help.